The Palace of Illusions

KIM ADDONIZIO

The Palace of Illusions

• STORIES •

SOFT SKULL PRESS • BERKELEY • AN IMPRINT OF COUNTERPOINT

Library of Congress Cataloging-in-Publication Data
Addonizio, Kim, 1954–
[Short stories. Selections]
The palace of illusions : stories / Kim Addonizio.
pages ; cm.
ISBN 978-1-59376-542-2
I. Addonizio, Kim, 1954– Beautiful Lady of the Snow.
II. Title.
PS3551.D3997A6 2014
813'.54'—dc23
2014014014

Cover design by Debbie Berne
Interior design by Elyse Strongin, Neuwirth & Associates, Inc.

SOFT SKULL PRESS
An imprint of Counterpoint
www.softskull.com

Printed in the United States of America

Distributed by Publishers Group West

10 9 8 7 6 5 4 3 2 1

For Aya

CONTENTS

BEAUTIFUL LADY OF THE SNOW 1

ONLY THE MOON 23

BREATHE 41

THE OTHER WOMAN 49

NIGHT OWLS 57

THE PALACE OF ILLUSIONS 83

IN THE TIME OF THE BYZANTINE EMPIRE 111

BLOWN 121

THE HAG'S JOURNEY 129

EVER AFTER 137

INTUITION 157

ANOTHER BREAKUP SONG 185

CANCER POEMS 191

ICE 221

ACKNOWLEDGMENTS 241

ABOUT THE AUTHOR 243

The Palace of Illusions

BEAUTIFUL LADY OF THE SNOW

Annabelle puts her hand in the water and scoops out one of the goldfish she got at the county fair. The other one leaves its little red and green castle to float up against the glass and watch. The fish flips over a few times on the counter. Annabelle doesn't want to hurt it; she only wants to stroke the shiny gold with her finger. But the fish flips so hard it sails off and lands on the floor next to her shoes, the new black patent-leather ones she got for First Communion. It doesn't look gold anymore, down in the shadows by the cupboard. She picks it up; it is quick and alive in her hand, its mouth opening and closing, trying to suck in air. Suddenly it wriggles free, flying away. She steps back, startled, and feels it squish under her heel.

She squats down to look. The head is flattened, a little liquid oozing from it. She gets a paper towel and crumples it around the fish, the way she has done with spiders. Then she puts it in the trash can under the sink, hiding it beneath a coffee filter full of wet grounds.

When Annabelle's mother comes into the apartment from the motel office, Annabelle is sitting on the couch with her feet straight out, watching TV over the shiny tops of her shoes. She wears them in the apartment all the time; her mother doesn't want her to scuff them by wearing them outside, except on special occasions.

Annabelle's mother manages the motel, and they get a free apartment behind the office. Annabelle's mother also has to take care of Grandpa, who lives in a trailer a few miles away and needs to go everywhere in a wheelchair with an oxygen tank. Grandpa can walk, when he needs to, but it is easier for him to ride, Annabelle's mother explained. Sometimes Grandpa makes Annabelle ride on his lap, and Annabelle hates that, hates sinking into the fat thighs, the smothering arms wrapped around her. Plus, he smells like an old cigar. Even though he is not supposed to smoke anymore, she knows he sits in a green plastic chair outside his trailer and does just that. The cigar butts are right there, in a Maxwell House can, and it is filled nearly to the top.

There are two good things about Grandpa's place. One is the white cat that lives in the woods behind his trailer, that will run up to eat the food Annabelle sets out for it on a napkin, as long as Annabelle stands far enough back. The other is that Grandpa will let Annabelle have sweets, though it is sort of a good and bad thing at the same time. Grandpa says he intends to spoil her rotten, and Annabelle understands this to mean that one day all the chocolates and Cokes and Oreos her grandfather has given her will turn her insides black and hollow, like the picture of a decayed tooth the dentist showed her. Not only her teeth are going to rot, but her whole body. Sometimes Grandpa will sneak a candy bar into her plastic Barbie purse, for later. It is a secret between them, something her mother doesn't know.

"Lord in Heaven," her mother says, coming over to the couch to sit next to Annabelle. "I'm sweating like a pig." She is wearing a white sleeveless blouse and shorts that show the purple veins on her legs. Her face is splotched with red. She wipes it with a washcloth and then uses the washcloth on each armpit. The couch is old, the worn cushion sinking under her weight. Annabelle moves to the other cushion and draws her knees up. If her feet touch the floor, the scaly monster that lives under the couch will drag her under.

"Having fun, baby?" her mother says, touching Annabelle's hair.

Annabelle shrugs.

"At least you got the air-conditioning." The apartment is cool, but in the office there is only a big fan that turns back and forth, pushing the hot air around. Her mother licks her thumb, then uses it to rub at a spot of dried milk on Annabelle's chin. Annabelle scowls and tries to duck, but her mother holds her head firmly with one hand until the milk is gone.

"There," her mother says. "Now you're pretty."

This is what Grandpa says when Annabelle puts on makeup for him. She brushes on powder and blush and red lipstick and glittery blue or green eye shadow that he bought for her at Rite Aid. She holds her long hair up like a glamorous model, and he tells her to get herself a piece of chocolate from the refrigerator, and to pour him some of his Ballantine whiskey. She twists the ice out of its tray carefully, into the freezer bin, and refills the tray. Then she puts three ice cubes in the glass and fills the glass. She chooses a chocolate, taking a few minutes to decide, trying to guess which one is the caramel and which is the cherry or the coconut or, best of all, the one with more chocolate inside. If she dances for Grandpa she will get another piece, and if she brings him a second glass of whiskey he will go to sleep, and she can eat whatever she likes.

It is the end of July, a month before second grade. In June Annabelle went to day camp, where she went swimming in a pool and made several ceramic ashtrays with lopsided scallops. But camp was too expensive to go for the whole summer. Now she has nothing to do all day but sit in the air-conditioning and watch TV, the curtains closed against the hot bright sun. Or she can play in a corner of the lobby with her Barbies, while the phone rings and grownups go in and out asking for the plastic cards that open the doors or pouring themselves coffee from the pot that sits on a burner all day next to the rack of brochures for the caverns. The caverns are the big attraction here, the only thing around that people might want to see, though Annabelle has never been there. The brochures show damp stalactites and rock walls that have folds in them like blankets. The visitors' children kick at the chairs in the lobby or grab handfuls of brochures and stare at her. They take butterscotch candies from the dish on the counter, which she is not allowed to have, filling their mouths and their pockets and dropping the wrappers on the floor. Annabelle is not allowed to pick up the wrappers, because they have germs. According to her mother, germs are everywhere, waiting to make you sick.

Annabelle is allowed to go behind the counter and sit at the big desk but not to answer the phone. She has a plastic one that she puts on the desk. She picks up the pink receiver and answers, "Burnside Motel," in a professional voice. She pretends her Old Maid cards are key cards, and she hands them out to her Barbies and tells them how to get to the different rooms and where they should park their cars. She explains that there are three places to eat in town—a Denny's, an Arby's, and Sue's Kitchen—and that Denny's has the best hamburgers but Sue's has really good fried chicken.

"Do you want to come sit with me in the office?" her mother says.

"Nope," Annabelle says. The TV show is interesting, cartoon mice in their furnished mouse hole with its arched doorway, backing away from a big orange cat's paw that is poking in. Annabelle holds her breath for a second, but the cat can't get to them.

"Mommy," she says. "Can I get a mouse?"

"A mouse! Hell, no. Mice are dirty. They carry germs."

"I want one," Annabelle says, jutting out her lower lip.

"You want a mouse," her mother says. "And what if the mouse gets loose? What if it runs into the office, or one of the rooms? We'll be out on our asses in ten minutes. No way you are getting a mouse, Missy."

On TV, the mice are tiptoeing into the kitchen, toward a big wedge of swiss cheese in a mousetrap.

"What about a gerbil?" Annabelle says.

• • •

7

Annabelle doesn't remember her father, who left when she was a baby. The man she thinks of as her father is the one who lived with them when she was in preschool and kindergarten and part of first grade. It's Joe she remembers, standing at the open kitchen window blowing smoke out into the white-flowered bushes bordering the motel, putting his cigarettes out one by one in the seashell ashtray on the sill. Joe used to read to her—stories about how the leopard got its spots and the loon got its necklace. He fixed the things that broke at the motel, the bathtub drains that clogged and the heaters that wouldn't come on. Now another man does that, but he doesn't live with them. Joe left, and there hasn't been anybody since, because, as Annabelle's mother explained to her, most men are good for nothing pieces of shit, who can't appreciate a quality woman.

Since Joe left, her mother has gotten almost as big as Grandpa. There are no sweets in the house, but there is lots of bread, kaiser rolls and English muffins and loaves of Wonder. There are boxes of macaroni and cheese that come in spirals or rounds, and family-sized bags of Fritos and pretzels and Ruffles and Pringles. Her mother can eat a whole tube of Pringles just during *Wheel of Fortune*. She snacks all day long in the office, too. At night, when she thinks Annabelle is asleep, she cries.

Annabelle lies in bed holding Simba, her stuffed lion, listening to her mother's sobbing. Usually Simba can comfort her, but tonight he seems indifferent to her troubles—her fears of rotting all over from too much candy, or of burning in hell, where her mother says all the bad people burn, her worry about her mother who is going to die of loneliness unless a man touches her soon and she gets some loving. Tonight

Simba does not seem to care that as each day passes there is no man and no loving and her mother is one step closer to dying. Simba is king of the jungle, the most powerful animal, and he can do anything when he wants to.

"Help," Annabelle whispers, but Simba seems to be sleeping. Annabelle hears her mother hang up the phone, then the crackle of a chip bag being opened. She puts both hands around Simba's neck and squeezes hard, but his eyes just shine at her blankly and she knows he is not going to come out from behind them.

. . .

It's a few days before Annabelle's mother notices that there is only one fish in the bowl on the kitchen counter. It is Annabelle's job to feed the fish; every morning and evening she has been shaking the flakes of food onto the surface of the water and watching the remaining one rise to the surface, its mouth open and working to catch them.

"Where's the other one?" her mother says one morning.

Annabelle shrugs, trying to be casual. She lifts a spoonful of Cheerios carefully to her mouth. Inside her chest, she can feel her heart flipping like the fish did, before she squashed it. She would like to tell her mother what happened, but maybe her mother will get mad, and then she will shake Annabelle, hard, spank her, and send her to her room.

"It flew away, I guess," she says.

"Well," her mother says, "I'm surprised they lived this long. Those things usually go belly-up in a week."

"Oh," Annabelle says. Her heart quiets, floating.

When her mother goes into the office, Annabelle returns to the bowl. She puts her index finger to the glass, and the fish swims to it, looking at her.

"Here, fishie," Annabelle says.

It swims away, returns. In a video Annabelle watched last night, a whale was captured and put in an aquarium, and then some children helped it get back to the ocean. She doesn't know where the ocean is, though, only that it's far away from here. She goes into the living room and sits on the couch for a few minutes, but she keeps thinking about the fish. She turns on the TV to distract herself, but the kitchen counter is just beyond the TV, and all she can see are the gold fins waving back and forth, the small beads of its eyes looking at her, asking her to set it free.

She thinks a minute, then goes over and climbs up on a stool. She takes the bowl in both hands, moving slowly so the water won't slosh over the sides, and carries it into the bathroom. She sets it on the floor and reaches her hand in and takes out the little castle. Then she dumps the water and the goldfish into the toilet bowl. She watches it swim around there, then goes to watch TV for a while and forgets about it.

When she has to pee, though, she remembers. She goes in and pulls down her jeans and underwear, and sits on the toilet. But she is afraid the fish will jump up and bite her vagina, maybe even swim up in there, so she gets up and flushes the toilet, making sure the fish is gone before she sits back down. She takes the bowl back to the kitchen, fills it with water from the sink, and puts the little castle back in the center. It will be a day or two, probably, before her mother notices, and then she can say it went belly-up and she had to throw it away.

. . .

Annabelle and her mother and Grandpa are at the Walmart, getting a new wooden folding table so Grandpa can sit on the couch and eat in front of the TV the way he likes to. He fell over the old one and broke it. He is always breaking things, dropping dishes, falling over furniture.

Annabelle's mother pushes the wheelchair while Annabelle walks behind them. She drifts back farther and farther, stopping to examine a wooden mousetrap that looks just like the one in the cartoon, only without the cheese. There are roach motels and ant powder, cans of Raid and Black Flag. Annabelle has seen her mother spray the lines of ants that sometimes crawl in, along the floor and up the wall; when she finishes, the ants are dark specks her mother wipes away, and the air smells sticky and sweet.

When Annabelle looks up, her mother and Grandpa have turned the corner. She heads to the part of the store she likes best, where the finches and parakeets are. The birds live in a big, square mesh cage with several trapezes for them to perch on. She likes the bright colors of their feathers and the sounds they make and their round black eyes that reflect the fluorescent lights of the store. She loses track of time, watching them. Then the loudspeaker calls a Code Adam, which Annabelle knows from a TV movie means that the employees are supposed to look around for an unattended child. In less than a minute a boy with a shaved head and dirty fingernails is there, dragging her up front to the checkout counters. Her mother is standing with her arms crossed against her chest, looking angry at the world. Grandpa is asleep in his chair.

"You scared the crap out of me," her mother says in her quiet voice that is scarier than her loud voice. She kneels down to take Annabelle by the shoulders and starts shaking her. "Look at me, dammit."

Annabelle shifts her gaze to the ground, focusing on her mother's sandaled feet, on the chipped scarlet polish of her toes. She feels that if her mother looks into her eyes, she'll be able to see the two goldfish, swirling around there the way the second one did before it was sucked down into the toilet bowl. She will be able to see Annabelle in her Little Mermaid underwear, made up like a model and dancing for Grandpa, her face and hands smeared with chocolate.

Finally she thinks of something she saw on a different TV movie. She looks into her mother's face and says, "I am fatherless."

. . .

Annabelle names the parakeet Sam. Her mother bought it for her that day, and they even stopped at the Dairy Queen on the way home. Sam is blue and green and yellow. He sits in his cage on the coffee table during the day, chirping and ringing a little bell, and at night Annabelle puts the plastic flowered cover over the cage.

"Now, isn't that better than a gerbil?" her mother says.

"I don't know," Annabelle says. "Can I still have one? Can I have a cat?" She thinks about the white cat that lives in the woods near Grandpa. It is a thin, bony thing that slinks out from the trees and streaks away if she moves toward it. She has named it Snowbelle, which means Beautiful Lady of the Snow, even though she doesn't know if it's a boy or girl. It hasn't let her get close enough.

At church that Sunday the priest talks about the Holy Spirit. There's the Father, the Son, and the Holy Spirit. The Father is away in heaven, and the Son died for everyone's sins, and the Holy Spirit is a dove that flies around, and comes down into you where you have an empty jar inside you, and it fills up your jar. If you don't get the Holy Spirit, you are a sinner and will burn up in hell. Annabelle imagines that hell looks like the caverns she has never seen, filled with dark damp spaces and black bats with fangs flying upside down trying to bite her face off. But there is something thrilling about hell, too, about the idea of going down deep inside a cave and not coming back up, hiding down there where no one can find her, where she can live by a river that looks and tastes like Coke, and all her Barbies will lie naked in a circle around her because she is the Queen Beautiful Lady Anna, and the pieces of shit men will be there and won't be able to leave because they are chained-up slaves. And if Joe is stuck down there she will use a big bucket to pour water on him so the flames don't hurt so much.

But what if Grandpa is there, too, with his oxygen tank, wetting his pants? Annabelle looks around the church. She needs to get the Holy Spirit right away. But all she sees are the pews filled with people, and light through the stained glass windows above them, and Jesus hanging on the big cross in his diaper, looking like he is asleep.

After church they go to Sue's Kitchen for lunch. Annabelle is wearing her pink dotted Swiss dress and Communion shoes, and her mother is dressed up and has used rollers in her hair so it has waves in it. Her mother orders Salisbury steak and gravy. Annabelle gets fried chicken and is allowed to have lime Jello for dessert. She drinks her milk with a straw, blowing pale white bubbles into the glass.

"What a sweet little angel," someone says.

Annabelle looks up. A man is standing next to their booth, a big pink-cheeked man with a neat black beard and no hair on his head. He has large, fleshy lips that make her think of the wax ones the Walmart sells at Halloween.

"She sure is a beauty," the man says, but he is looking at her mother, not Annabelle. He leans both hands on their table, meaty hands with big hairy knuckles and long fingers and— she counts them quickly—six rings.

"Sweet!" her mother says. "Stubborn as a mule, is what she is."

Annabelle is surprised by how her mother says it; her voice is soft as a melted butter pat.

"Her mother ain't bad, neither," the man says. His voice is a butter knife, slipping in easily, smearing the butter around on soft bread.

Annabelle slides down the back of the leather booth until her feet are way under the table and her head is on the seat, and squinches her eyes shut.

"You raising her alone?" the man says.

"With God's help."

This is the first Annabelle has heard about God helping out.

"I can't say I'm a believer, myself," the man says, "though

sometimes I figure there must be something else out there. I mean, all that space, there's got to be, right? Even if it's only little green men with bug eyes."

Annabelle's mother laughs, and Annabelle pictures green men the size of ants, crawling out of an anthill.

"I envy those who have faith," the man says.

"Well, to each his own," her mother says. "I believe everyone should get along."

"I wouldn't mind getting along with you," the man says, and Annabelle thinks about the green man-ants swarming up the ramp into Grandpa's trailer, crawling along his wheelchair and into his eyes and nose and ears, starting to eat him alive.

The man stands there talking to her mother for what seems like forever.

"I have to pee," Annabelle says. Her mother just waves her hand, so Annabelle goes by herself. When she comes out, the man is gone. She follows her mother out to their van.

"He's going to come by the motel," her mother says. "He usually stays at the Days Inn, but they don't have free HBO like we do, and all they serve for breakfast are bad donuts, and we have those cinnamon buns from Sue's. Do you want one tomorrow? You can have one tomorrow." Her mother babbles on, the way she did when she was taking those green and white pills to help her stop eating. They didn't work; she just ate and talked all day and cried harder at night.

When they get to the motel her mother goes back to work in the dress she wore to church, instead of changing into sweatpants and a T-shirt like she usually does, and Annabelle leans forward on the couch looking at Sam in his cage, poking her finger in to touch him.

. . .

The man comes that night, through the door at the back of the office and into their apartment. Annabelle spies on them from her bedroom, her door cracked open. They are on the couch together, laughing. The man has on a T-shirt, thick dark hair all down his fat arms. One dark, ugly arm is around her mother's shoulders. Her mother lets her head fall back, and the man pours beer from the bottle into her mouth.

"Atta girl," he says. "Shit, you can hold it."

Her mother sits up, reaches for a bottle on the table. There are a lot of bottles. Her mother's legs are open, her dress hiked up. Annabelle watches the man put his own beer on the floor, watches his hand disappear under her mother's dress. Her mother squirms, then pulls his hand away.

"Not here," she says. "My kid—"

"She's asleep," he says. He unzips his pants, leans close to her ear, and says something.

"You're filthy," Annabelle's mother says.

Annabelle thinks about filthy germs.

But her mother is laughing. "Not now," she says. "Later—"

"Okay," the man says. He reaches for his beer on the floor and knocks it over. "Hell," he says. "Sorry about that." He looks at Sam's cage on the table, the plastic cover over it. He pulls the cover off.

"Where's the bird?" he says.

. . .

Annabelle is being punished for letting Sam out of his cage. She is not allowed to watch TV for three days. She told her mother that she wanted Sam to be free. She didn't tell her that he had bitten her finger, that she had unlatched the door and put her hand in to grab him, then run to the bathroom sink and turned the water all the way on and stuck him under the faucet. She felt his small body, his heart beating frantically in her hand.

"You're bad," she told him. "You're bad and you have to be punished."

He struggled and thrashed in the water, splashing her face and arms.

"I think you're sorry now," she said. "I think you're sorry and don't need to be punished anymore. And just remember, don't try to fly away."

But when she lifted him up he wouldn't move. She patted him with a dry washcloth, but he stayed sodden and still. She wrapped him in the washcloth and rocked him back and forth. Finally she carried him outside in her pink Barbie purse and buried him around the side of the motel where she isn't supposed to go, where there is nothing but a field of dead grass and an abandoned gas station where the high school kids leave empty beer cans and candy wrappers and cigarette butts.

Now Sam will be with her in hell, by the river where the goldfish will swim back and forth like tiny flickering pieces of fire. There is no way she will get the Holy Spirit now. She doesn't care about not watching TV; she sits in her room, holding Simba, rocking him the way she did with Sam. Simba knows all about Grandpa, but he won't help her.

In the afternoon she runs errands for her mother, brings her Diet Mountain Dew and Fritos from the apartment, and by the end of the day her mother has forgiven her.

The man is in room 220, just upstairs from them. No one ever stays here more than a night. They check in one day, and the next day they are gone, to someplace where there is more to see than some caves in the ground.

"You're staying at Grandpa's tonight," her mother tells her.

When the night clerk, Jolie, shows up to relieve her mother, Annabelle has packed her pajamas and toothbrush and clean underwear and Simba and two Barbies in a plastic bag. Her Barbie purse is over her shoulder. In the purse is a tube of Cherry Chapstick, a pair of yellow sunglasses with daisies on them, some butterfly hair clips, and one blue feather that belonged to Sam.

On the drive over her mother talks nonstop about the man, whose name is Jim. Jim is a hoot. Jim likes to watch baseball and hockey. Jim sells office supplies right now but he could sell anything, anywhere, even something here in this town. Jim is a miracle from heaven, God has finally heard her prayers, and Annabelle should pray that he stays so she will no longer be a fatherless little girl.

Annabelle doesn't want to pray. Jim isn't her father; Joe was, but Joe has gone and she doesn't know where. When he left, he forgot to say good-bye; she had watched his pickup turn out of the parking lot, and waited for him to remember and turn around, the way he often turned around because he had forgotten his glasses, or forgot he didn't have any money to take her for an ice cream and had to go back and get some from her mother. Sometimes they would get as far as Denny's before he remembered, and he would whip a U-turn in the middle of the road and then she would run in and get the glasses or money or his cigarettes, and run back to the truck. Maybe Joe will remember one day that he forgot Annabelle, and will come back for her in his truck that smells like cigarettes and air freshener, and they will go away and be married.

"I don't want to go to Grandpa's," Annabelle says, as soon as her mother pulls out onto the road.

"Tough titties, baby," her mother says. "Your old mother's got a date."

"He smokes cigars," Annabelle says. "I think they have germs." She tries to think of what else she can say, to get her mother to turn the car around.

"Those cigars are going to kill him for sure," her mother says.

The trees go by on both sides of the road. They are tall, so tall it's hard to see the top of them. Annabelle wishes she were a tree, with her feet planted firmly in the dirt behind the motel and her head sticking into heaven.

"I dance for him," Annabelle says finally.

She wants to take it back as soon as she says it, because her mother's face changes right away, and she pulls off abruptly into a gravel turnoff and jams on the brakes.

"What do you mean?" her mother says. "What do you mean, you dance for him?"

"Nothing," Annabelle says, looking down into her lap.

Her mother has her by the shoulders. "You dance for him," her mother repeats.

"Is it a sin?" Annabelle says.

She thinks about doing the hula in front of Grandpa, to the music she has to imagine in her head. She thinks about her arms moving from side to side, like waves in the ocean, wherever it is. She thinks of climbing into a boat that is too small for Grandpa and his wheelchair. A whale will tow her out to sea, a rope from the boat looped around its tail.

"I do the hula," she says.

"Oh," her mother says, looking into her eyes.

But Annabelle feels, now, that her mother can't see anything there, that she probably doesn't want to see anything—not the fish, not Sam, and not Grandpa watching her dance, drinking his whiskey.

"Be careful," her mother says.

"Yes, ma'am," Annabelle says.

●　●　●

At Grandpa's, Annabelle watches whatever Grandpa watches; tonight it is one of the crime shows he likes. There is a little girl about Annabelle's age, but she isn't really in the show, only her picture; she has disappeared, and the police are trying to find her, talking to different grownups and to the girl's teen-aged babysitter.

A commercial comes on, a big expensive car going fast down a highway toward some mountains in the distance.

"Fix me another drink," Grandpa says.

He has been saying this for a while now, drinking fast. Annabelle hopes that means he is going to fall asleep soon. She goes and makes him another one. She sees the new box of chocolates in the refrigerator when she opens the freezer for ice.

"How about a little dance from my girl?" Grandpa says, when she brings him his whiskey.

"It's my bedtime," Annabelle says, which it is. She is already in her pajamas. She yawns, opening her mouth wide, stretching her arms up.

"Aw, c'mon," Grandpa says. "Pretty please with Hershey's syrup on top."

"I don't like chocolate anymore," Annabelle says.

"Oh, sure you do," Grandpa says. "You love it. My favorite little girl," he says. "My little girl loves chocolate."

"No, I don't," Annabelle says.

"You listen to your Grandpa," he says. "Do what I tell you."

"No." She remembers her mother saying, *Stubborn as a mule* to the man in Sue's Kitchen. "I hate chocolate," she says. "And I hate dancing and I hate it when you wet your pants, so *there*."

Grandpa looks at her a moment. Then he says, "You spoiled little brat." He looks really upset. Annabelle has never seen him like this before. He has always been nice as pie, smiling at her, giving her treats and presents, asking her for dances. "Get over here right now." He starts to rise from the couch, but sinks back down, wheezing and red in the face.

"I need my oxygen," he says. His tank is in the bedroom. "Go bring it in here."

"No," Annabelle says.

"Now!" Grandpa says.

This is a Grandpa she has never seen, angry and needing his oxygen.

"I won't," Annabelle says.

"Oh, yes you will, Missy."

He is breathing more slowly now, his face returning to its normal color. Again, he starts to get up from the couch. But before he is even off it, she has run out the door of the trailer and down the ramp.

"Get back here," Grandpa calls.

But Grandpa is old, and slow. By the time he is at the door, she is running through the woods in the dark, branches stinging her face and arms.

When she can't run anymore she stops, panting. She looks back toward the trailer, at a light pole on the road she knows is nearby. She can't actually see the trailer, or Grandpa. Maybe he has gone back to get his tank from the bedroom, to sit on the couch and watch his show. Or maybe he is in the plastic chair in the dirt yard, smoking one of his cigars. The cigars will kill him one day. Her mother said so. Every day, Grandpa will get older and slower, and Annabelle will get bigger and stronger. If he chases her, Grandpa will wheeze and turn red in the face. The next time he asks for his oxygen, she will hide it, and he won't be able to catch his breath. He will take in the air in little gasps, and then he will pass out for good, and be perfectly still. Then Annabelle will disappear, like the girl on the crime show. No one will be able to find out where she is. She will live in the woods in a fort, just her and Simba and the white cat Beautiful Lady of the Snow. Annabelle has never seen real snow, but she knows that somewhere, like at the North Pole, it falls all the time, covering the ground and trees and buildings, making everything it touches white, and pure again.

ONLY THE MOON

It's Halloween, and I don't have plans with anyone. No big thing. It's only a Wednesday evening. From Sunday through Wednesday, if I happen to be alone in front of my old Sony TV with a succession of gin-and-tonics and a diminishing package of salt-and-vinegar potato chips, this is not a serious existential problem. After Wednesday, though, things get dicier. First there is Thursday, or "little Friday": the bars and restaurants crowded, the clubs pulsing with music and bodies until the dawn hours. If little Friday arrives and I don't have plans, a sharp but still-distant note of anxiety begins to sound—the harsh whistle of a train, coming from a long way off. On Friday it rumbles closer, and on Saturday night it appears from around the curve and bears down on me, huge and monstrous, threatening to cut me in two.

So, it's only Wednesday. But Halloween complicates things: a day of bank tellers in bunny ears and fairy wings, the occasional drunken clown reeling from a bar at lunch hour with a smeared red smile, so that by evening the air is charged with the lonely ions of expectation. It is not a night to stay in, watching ill-trained teenaged actors get cut up with knives or crushed under electric garage doors or chased sobbing through the woods. I call three different friends, but everyone else has had the foresight to find a date, and no one invites me to tag along. Next I call Mona. Mona is way older, like sixty or so, and she hasn't dated in years.

"Let's go for drinks," Mona says. "I was going to have dinner, but I'll skip it. Nothing like a liquid diet."

I can hear ice slithering around in a glass, and behind that her TV going. Predictably, someone is screaming. Nearly every channel has some kind of scare-a-thon happening.

"Drinks it is, then," I say.

"I'll just finish my drink," Mona says, "and get ready."

"Your pre-drink, you mean. Before we have drinks."

"I get thirsty this time of day."

"Always."

All my friends are drinkers. Most Fridays we gather after work at some bar, then go to dinner and order carafe after carafe of house red. In my circle, the parties last long—until the revelers slip to the floor or stagger off to pass out on a neighbor's lawn, maybe climbing into their cars, if they have them, to wend their erratic way home through the deserted streets. We start the weekend mornings with a Bloody Mary or Mimosa or Ramos Fizz, with Walprofen and Aleve and Excedrin, with groans and nausea that gradually slide into hilarity. We get through our McJobs with flasks, and have beer with lunch. We head out of Starbucks and Kinko's and financial district offices for fifteen-minute cocktail binges on our scheduled breaks. Forget AA. AA is for losers who can't handle their shit.

"Let's go to the Redwood Room at the Clift," Mona says. "I haven't seen it since it's been renovated."

On her TV, a girl's voice goes, *Oh, God, no. Oh, God, please, no, no.*

"Pick you up in an hour," I say.

"I'll treat, of course. But make it sooner. I don't want any fucking little kids at my door."

Mona always treats me. She has that appealing combination of wealth and carelessness with money. Hundred-dollar bills spill from her Italian leather wallet. She's big on cashmere coats; she owns five. Gucci and Fendi bags, Ferragamo shoes, Dior scarves—Mona always looks like she stepped out of a photo shoot, materializing into the air on a breath of floral perfume from a fashion magazine. Her hair is white-blonde, sleek and smooth as metal, and falls straight to her shoulders. Her eyes are a color of blue that looks like it has metal in it, too. Mona exudes an aura of ease and luxury, of eternal impossible beautiful moments in exotic locations where even the inanimate objects, like chaise lounges and sea walls, admire your flawlessness.

In honor of Halloween I put on a long leopard-print skirt with slits on each side up to mid-thigh, and a black velvet bustier with leather laces. For good measure I wear my black hat with the square of lace hanging down the back and the fake roses on the brim, and slather on the makeup. I drink a quick toast before I leave, a cold shot of Estonian vodka raised to dodging the bullet of sitting at home in my bathrobe, in thrall to scenes of a couple being terrorized by a doll in overalls. I've been transformed into a sexy twenty-seven-year-old jungle cat out on the prowl, ready for whatever magic the night may bring. When I get in my car, a guy in a George Bush mask whistles, and his friend, encased in an alien creature with eyes the size of tennis balls, meows at me.

At the Redwood Room I get a Clift Cosmopolitan, and Mona a Manhattan. I don't know anybody who drinks Manhattans except Mona. I feel like I should have ordered something more classic, like a martini. There's a purple flower floating in my drink that the waitress identifies as a pansy; she tells us it's edible.

Though I'm kind of hungry from not having any dinner, I don't think a pansy or two will make a difference, so I just pluck it out and set it on my napkin.

The waitress looks about my age, a slim thing in a sleeveless black dress with a tattoo of Chinese characters running down the back of one bare shoulder. She says they mean, "only the moon." As in, only the moon will do.

"It's all about following your dreams," she says.

"Follow your bliss," I say. "Joseph Campbell said that."

"How perfectly lovely," Mona says, sipping her drink. When the waitress goes, she leans toward me. "Pushing drinks in an overpriced hotel bar," she says. "Dreams, my ass."

"She probably makes ten times more than me." I look around the room and think that's probably true of everyone in here.

"That's right, you work," Mona says, like she's forgotten this distasteful fact. "Please let's talk about something more scintillating than Starbucks."

"Colloquially known as Starfucks," I say.

"Star fucking. There's a promising subject. Would you fuck Brad Pitt?"

"Under what circumstances?"

"That qualifies as a no."

Mona starts rattling off actors' names, but my mind is on the waitress and her tattoo. I know I'm not exactly following my bliss. It's more like the path of least resistance. I went from counter help to shift supervisor, from making lattes and Frappuccinos to making sure people take their breaks on time and the store stays picked up and the right hot sleeves for the cups get ordered. Health benefits and everything, but come on.

"Leo DiCaprio," Mona says. "Will Smith. Robert Pattinson."

It's not inconceivable that one of them could walk into the Redwood Room. The Redwood Room is the hip place to go since the trendy hotelier bought the Clift and put his trendy stamp on a San Francisco institution. The walls are paneled from a single two-thousand-year-old redwood, the bar is U-shaped and seventy-five feet long, the chandeliers and wall sconces are deco. He's added a few touches, like a glass bar and plasma-screen images of Klimt paintings to replace the ones that used to hang there. When we arrived it was busy enough, but now the room's seething with people. Every seat is taken, except for a row of them at a long low table, another trendy addition. People keep trying to sit there, on glass stools that look like vases, but after an uncomfortable minute they get up and go over to stand by one of the bars.

We're at the U-shaped one, people jammed in on both sides. Mona has given up on pimping me to movie stars and has struck up an acquaintance with the guy across from her. Pretty soon he's offering her shrimp cocktail and french fries off his plate. He's a salesman staying at a different hotel who just came here for dinner, he says, but I can tell he was secretly hoping to meet some willing young thing he could take back to his room and fuck the life out of. He's in a nice suit he probably saved for tonight, and the cologne is rolling off him in nauseating waves. I bet there's a wedding ring sitting on the sink in his hotel room, that he had to soap off his pudgy finger.

Across from me, there's a different kind of guy. He's my age, or maybe a little younger—he has baby skin, not a line on it, and a sparse blond goatee that looks like it's been trying to grow in since eighth grade. He's hunched over the bar, wearing a faded T-shirt with a faded Spiderman leaping on it, his shoulder bones sticking out like a famine victim's. There's a barely touched glass of beer in front of him. In the middle of the Redwood Room, surrounded by dressed-up people laughing and getting shitfaced, he's reading *The Portable Nietzsche*. Right away I figure I know things about him, like that he doesn't own a car, but feels superior to people who do. He labors at some shit office job, maybe even temp work, and writes bad poetry nobody understands. He's got poser written all over him, but he's got nice eyes, pale blue or maybe gray, fringed by the kind of sweeping lashes any girl would kill for. By now I have three damp pansies arranged on my napkin from the drinks I've had, and I'm feeling friendly. Also hungry. I can feel the alcohol traveling around my stomach, looking for a scrap of food to connect to, to lose itself in. I take a couple of chilly shrimp from the salesman's plate without asking, knowing he won't say anything.

"Hey, Nietzsche," I say to the poser, by way of an opener. "Thou shalt." I remember a little of my Nietzsche—the golden-scaled dragon in *Thus Spake Zarathustra* who's like the superego, telling you all the things you're supposed to do to fit in, promoting the decadent values of Christian civilization. I majored in Philosophy in college. I kept meaning to take the GREs and go to grad school so I could teach, but year after year I lost my nerve. By now there are only a few bits and pieces. The Sophists, for example. I can't remember which one argued that might is right, which one contrasted law and nature. Dewey's critique of traditional philosophy is a total blank.

"Excuse me?" he says, and takes his time looking up.

The thing is, he's been watching me for I don't know how long. I didn't even notice him when he first sat down, but a while ago I felt him stealing looks over the top of his beer while pretending to be absorbed in his book. He'd started out with it flat on the bar, but little by little he raised it, until I could see the title and know what a brilliant superior intellectual he was.

"I hope you don't take him seriously," I said.

He gives me a contemptuous look. "Oh, right," he says. "God forbid we should touch on anything *serious*."

"That's not what I meant." I glance at the salesman, who pushes a french fry suggestively into a blob of ketchup. I feel the shrimp sliding down into my stomach, tossing cold and forlorn on a turbulent sea. I'm thinking I should have stayed home after all. I could have rented *Dawn of the Dead* and watched zombies stagger around the mall.

"What I meant," I say, "is that if you take him too seriously, you end up being a menace to society. All that superman and will to power stuff. The idea you can make up your own rules, that conventional standards of good and evil don't apply." I'm impressed with how much I suddenly remember. For a minute I see myself in front of a podium in a large auditorium, rows of students taking down every word I say. On everyone's desk, my book *On Moral Life* is open, passages highlighted in fluorescent yellow.

"Ah," he says, "a fellow philosopher." He's turned his book face down on the bar, but in case that's giving me too much credit, he leans back away from me on his stool.

"Not really. I majored in it. In a previous life."

"And what do you do in this incarnation?" He's still leaning back, trying to be cool, but I bet anything his hands are sweating. I bet he can't believe he's met a woman who actually knows something about his precious Nietzsche. He's probably, in his mind, already got me naked on his mattress on the floor in the crummy apartment he shares with four other losers.

"Guess," I say.

"Stripper?" he says hopefully.

"No."

"Model," he says. "Caterer. Lawyer. Dot-Commer. Artist."

"No. No, no, no, no. No." He has no clue who I might be. I give Mona a look, but for some reason she's amused by the pervy salesman, and she shakes her head.

"I'm a demon," I say. "I steal infants from their cribs, drain the life out of men as they sleep. That kind of thing."

"Perfect," he says. "I'm a warlock."

More drinks have appeared. I look around at the walls, and where the bright, glittery plasma images of Klimt paintings were, there are now portraits of solemn men and women in dark tailored jackets, who look like they're presiding over a board meeting. I look at one of the men, and his eyes slowly blink. Mona nudges me.

"Drink up," she says, "we're moving the party."

. . .

One thing about Mona. She has bad judgment. The night we met, she announced this to a group of people at a party, and I immediately wanted to know her. I went over and struck up a conversation, and we ended up sitting on the floor in a corner of the room, doing shots of Añejo tequila. That night Mona slept on the couch, and I passed out naked in the host's guest bedroom with his friend from out of town, who later credited my blow job with helping him leave his bad marriage. Tequila, as everyone knows, is a dangerous substance. Just last week, after a night of doing shots of Margaritaville, I woke up bleeding from the wrong part of my anatomy and had to call a friend to take me to the Emergency Room. After waiting an hour to be seen we gave up and went to get some wine. Going to this guy's room is probably an error in judgment. But that's where we're headed—me, Mona, Don the salesman, and Nietzsche the warlock, who has introduced himself as Joseph.

We head down Geary Street two by two—me and Mona in front, arm in arm, the men following. That's how it is in nature: stallions nickering after mares, boring-colored male birds having to sing just to attract a mate. I'm savoring the moment, because usually I'm alienated from nature, sitting by the phone. My last date was with a loser named George who made me pay for dinner, and then demanded BART fare when I refused to drive him home across the Bay Bridge. The one before him—Jack? Zack?—was overmedicated, and about to be evicted by his roommates for not paying his share of the rent. For our date, we sat in his living room sharing cheap chianti and takeout pizza, while his roommates walked in and out muttering "Asshole" under their breath. His hands never stopped shaking the whole evening. I woke up beside him at four a.m., watched him twitch for a while, then went to find some Ibuprofen to kill my wine headache.

The streets are full of people, but no one's in costume. Women in short dresses and shimmery jackets, men in suits, homeless people saying "trick or treat" from doorways. Right now, in the Castro, men are mincing down the street in sequined gowns and tutus and leather chaps. In the Mission and Noe Valley, little gypsies and devils and ballerinas and hobbits are going door to door. Here on Geary Street it hardly feels like Halloween at all, but then we turn a corner and I see there's a full moon, huge and orange in the sky above the Bay Bridge. I'm beginning to feel like maybe the night's not as lost as I thought. Maybe Joseph will surprise me and turn out to have a real job and a live-work loft. He'll let me move in, and he'll selflessly support me through graduate school, disproving Nietzche's belief that all altruistic sentiment is cowardice. We'll tell our children how we met on Halloween under a full moon and they'll roll their eyes and say, *Mom. Dad. Not that one again.*

"Look at that moon," Mona says.

I wonder how she can sound so sober, when she's had as many drinks as me; sometimes Mona seems impervious to alcohol. I wonder if she has ever woken up hung over and depressed, and had to drag herself to a job she hates, and offer friendly, polite service to people who are stupider, shallower, and more successful than she is. I think not. She points to the moon with one elegant finger, her hair blazing in its light.

"Mona, you are a goddess," I say.

"We are in the company of goddesses," Joseph says, and I want to lick his face.

• • •

Here's what Hume thought: he thought that morality was basically utilitarian. We do things because they're useful, not because they're right. According to Hume, the rules get suspended when you don't need them. In war, for example, the rules go out the window. Rape, torture, indiscriminate murder—that's pretty much what happens in a war. Hume had other depressing things to say, too, like that our universe might be the fucked-up experiment of some retarded minor god. The god was probably blind drunk and messing around; he probably set our little planet spinning, slapped the first man on top of the woman like they were Ken and Barbie, and passed out. The next day his head was killing him and he'd completely forgotten what he'd done.

"Hume turned Plato on his head," I tell Joseph and pour myself more of the champagne Don ordered from room service. But then I can't remember how Hume turned Plato on

35

his head, only that my former professor said it, years ago. I was in love with him, the kind of love that leads to standing in the street screaming someone's name at their dark apartment building. When it stopped being useful to him to fuck me, he just changed his phone number and forgot I was alive.

"Here's my philosophy," Mona says. "Drink, drink, and be merry. For tomorrow we disappear like smoke." She's sitting in a striped chair, legs crossed, idly dangling one expensive high heel and exhaling perfect smoke rings. Mona smokes almost as much as she drinks.

"Carpe vino." I lift my glass and look through it at the hotel room, the walls and furniture wavering inside a tiny lake of champagne, and then I drain the lake. "How come you don't date, Mona?"

"Oh, men are such swine," she says.

"Not all of them," Don says from the queen bed. He's lying there like he's waiting for one of us to join him, stretched out with his feet in their thin black socks pointed at the ceiling.

"No," Mona says, "some of them are dogs."

"Arf!" Don says. "Arf arf arf!"

Joseph is reading his Nietzsche, sitting cross-legged on the floor. "Or is it this," he says, reading aloud. "To go into foul water when it is the water of truth."

"I need to be petted," Don says. "I'm a lonely puppy. Pet me, pet me," he says. He raises his arms like paws. He lets his tongue loll out and starts panting, fast and shallow.

"Women," Joseph says. "You always think you're better than us." He puts down his book and upends his glass, chugging his champagne, then looks around for more. I've set the last bottle with anything in it—there were three—on the night-stand next to Don. Joseph looks at me, like I'm supposed to get it for him.

"We *are* better than you," I say. "Look who starts all the wars. Who most of the serial killers are. The terrorists. The rapists."

"The dentists," Mona adds.

"You're all the same," Joseph says. He gets up and goes for the bottle. My glass is empty, too, but instead of filling it he takes the bottle and goes and sits back down on the floor with it.

"No, we're not." I go and sit next to him. "That's a mean thing to say. And it's also inaccurate."

"I'm sorry. I don't know why I said it. I'm an asshole. I say stupid things sometimes. Especially when I like somebody."

I take the bottle and pour myself some more. It takes some concentration to perform this act, as the rim of the champagne flute seems to have shrunk in diameter. "What do you like about me?"

"You're cool," Joseph says.

I lean in to kiss him. I move toward him like a bee aiming for a flower, an insect driven by instinct, not caring that the pollen dusting its feet will aid in the process of plant reproduction. Selfishness and intoxication propel me toward his slightly parted lips. Our tongues wrestle in the dark cave our mouths make, mashed together.

"Somebody get a hose," Mona says.

We kiss some more and then I pull away and look at him. His whole face is soft and open, like a flower that's just gorged itself on sunlight.

"Way cool," he says. "Definitely way cool."

"Do you know any other words?" Mona says.

"Mona, have you ever been married?" I ask her.

"I can't imagine anything more tedious," Mona says, "than marriage."

She finishes her cigarette and goes over to the window, where she's left her glass on the ledge. There are two Monas now, one in the room and another reflected in the window. Ideal Mona and Real Mona. Plato's world of forms—the phrase drifts through my head, a little boat headed for the horizon without anything like knowledge to anchor it. Now the world of forms is starting to double, too; Mona lifts her glass and there are two of her in the room, resolving into one when I blink, then doubling again. I close my eyes.

"To freedom," she says, "from giving a shit."

I try on Mona's idea, like I'm winding one of her expensive silk scarves around me. Marriage is tedious. I imagine growing old alone, forever raising a glass of champagne to not giving a shit.

"Pet me, pet me, pet me," Don says.

• • •

Don is snoring, if that's what you'd call the sounds he's making. He breathes out through his closed mouth, and a little air escapes, making a soft *pop-pop-pop* sound. I almost expect champagne bubbles to float out of him.

Joseph is gone. What happened to Joseph? We were arguing about something, I remember. *You think you're so superior,* he said. *Fuck off, then,* I said. I think I passed out for a while after that. I'm sprawled in a striped wing chair and I feel too high to move. I imagine Joseph riding home in the ghastly light of a Muni streetcar. All around him, partygoers in brightly colored costumes talk and laugh, heading for another party or for the festivities on Castro Street. He sits there lonely and bitter, his shoulders slumped, and I wish I'd given him my phone number.

Mona is leaning over Don, her back to me. It looks like she's taking off his pants. But then she stands up, and I see she's got his wallet. She pulls out the bills, and a silver credit card, then flips the wallet closed and sets it on the nightstand.

"Mona," I say.

She wiggles her hand behind her back, waving me away.

"You took his money."

"No shit," she says, straightening. She picks up her beaded clutch, clicks it open, and drops the money and credit card inside.

"You're stealing his money."

"I'm liberating it. Let's go. He looks dead to the world, but you never know."

"You're a thief," I say. Mona is a thief. I wonder how I could not have known before. It seems like the most natural thing in the world.

She comes over and pulls me up by one arm. I stagger and fall into her. Her perfume's too strong and she smells like all the cigarettes she's had, and I gag and taste the fries I ate earlier, rising on a tide of champagne.

"Wait." I go into the bathroom, squat down and crouch over the toilet, but nothing happens. I pull a hand towel off the rack, wet it under the faucet, and wipe my face. Don's ring is on the counter, just like I thought. It's there next to his electric toothbrush and a tube of mint Colgate he's been squeezing from the top instead of the bottom. I pick up the ring; it's a plain gold circle, and inside, in cursive, the name *Debbie* is engraved. I close it in my hand, and when I come out I slip it into my purse so fast Mona doesn't even notice.

We head out of the room and along the hall to the elevator. It's one of those mirrored ones. The walls below the mirrored part are dark wood, and the floor is thickly carpeted, and a brass railing runs all the way around. I look at us in the mirror as we descend, and Mona watches the numbers light as we go from *5* to *L.* We look like shit. The skin under Mona's eyes is pouchy, and there are small red veins in her cheeks where her foundation's worn off. My eyes are bloodshot, the lids drooping. I forgot my hat, and my hair is flattened and tangled.

In another couple of minutes we're through the lobby and out of the building, on the sidewalk, empty now except for a few shadowy bodies stretched out in doorways. We walk fast toward my car, our heels echoing and amplified, like we're on a movie set. The fog is in, and it looks like there's no sky at all, like the movie takes place in some damp underground world where the sun never shines. I know where we are, though. I can't see the moon, but I know it's out there somewhere, a well of light. I tell myself I could throw myself into it any time I wanted. I tell myself that, even though I know who I am.

BREATHE

Breathe in, the teacher—roshi, guru, leader, whatever—says, so, okay, so far, so good, deep breath, hold it, let it out on a long exhale. Amber, my roommate, smiles at me, like, *Isn't this going to be great, isn't California so cool?* and I look back like, *Yes it is,* even though I don't think so. Already my knees are bothering me from sitting cross-legged. We all take a few more deep, noisy breaths. We're supposed to close our eyes, but I peek around at the class, trying to spot someone cute who might want to talk to me later, until the teacher, woman, enlightened being, bitch, catches me, and her soft open eyes get hard, and I zip mine closed again.

Be still, she tells us. *Go inward.* She has some kind of accent I can't figure out. She sounds a little like that waitress in Montpelier, Vermont, where I spent Christmas with my parents. They didn't want to have Christmas at home in Florida anymore; they said it would be better if we were somewhere with snow. We stayed in a farmhouse, and it was really cold. My parents went tromping around through the woods in galoshes

43

and boots and cross-country skis, and I stayed in by the fire under a big quilt, feeling lonely and sad and fat. I felt like a big icicle was dripping inside me, without ever melting. So I don't want to go inward. Right now I want to go home, ignore my freshman comp homework, and curl up on the couch and watch *The Tudors*, the entire series, for the second time on Showtime On Demand. I want broken treaties and assassination plots and girl baby after girl baby being born to King Henry VIII, while he gets more and more desperate for a boy.

Watch your thoughts, the teacher says at this point, and I get that, that's easy; I just imagine my TV, a thirty-two-inch flat screen I got from Best Buy. I watch Amber telling me I should do something else besides eat and watch my new TV night and day, and then I watch her fill the fridge in our dorm apartment with probiotic ginseng drinks and baked tofu, and then I rummage around on my own shelf for some sugar cookies I baked and put in there to cool. I hate them warm from the oven. I will eat the dough all day long, though. That's bad, I guess, because raw eggs can infect you with salmonella, but if I die from eating raw cookie dough I don't think I'll mind; I'll just pitch over in our kitchen with a big smile.

So now I'm thinking about death. The death thought looks like a lump of buttery sugary dough and raisins, and then it looks like a shiny balloon that's starting to crinkle and sag, and then it's a baseball cap—a pink baseball cap just floating in space with no person in it. Then, as I watch, the cap falls sideways into a tunnel like it's being sucked out of my head, and my little sister, Bethany, appears in all her dead glory, or rather in the slide show my parents made of her afterwards, that we all watched projected on our living room wall when we got back from the cemetery. It's mostly pictures of her when she was healthy. There's one of us in our bathing suits at Lake Placid one summer, and another where we're posing with our Easter baskets, in bunny ears. There's only one of her from near the end. She's wearing lipstick and blue eye shadow and that baseball cap on her head, looking like Cancer Awareness Poster Girl, a goofy smile on her face, like she didn't throw up the morning our dad took the photo.

I don't really want to watch the slideshow in my head so I open my eyes again, just let them slowly part to tiny slits so the room looks fuzzy. The teacher, woman, skank, catches me again, so I open my eyes all the way and look straight at her and give her a gentle look, like *I'm all blissed out*, and she nods her head at me and closes her own eyes and opens them, like, *It's all good.* Which it is not, but here we are.

I must have given her some signal because she suddenly says, *Let's all chant some* Aums. Everyone tries to hold their *Aum* longer than everyone else and some people cheat, taking a second breath while other people are still letting out the first one. I get my *Aums* over with as fast as possible. All I want is to get out of here and go home and order a big gooey sausage-pepper-onion pizza from Red Boy and eat the whole thing in front of the TV. Anne Boleyn and Cardinal Wolsey are down with the sweating disease. They're going to recover from that, but they're done for, anyway. Wolsey will get arrested for treason and kill himself, and Anne will stand on the scaffolding bravely addressing the crowd, saying nice things about Henry, who ordered her head cut off. She's going to forgive the black-hooded guy with the sword, and kneel down and pray. She'll look up at the sky. Black birds will flap around for an instant in the blue. I really want to see that episode again.

But the class, torture session, boredom hour, has just begun.

With your eyes closed, says our guide, *simply watch your breath.* She says this looking straight at me, so I have no choice.

But how are you supposed to watch your breath? My breath doesn't look like anything. First I imagine my tongue is a road, and my breath is wind whooshing down from some black space in the back of my head, but I can't really see the wind. All I see is a long road disappearing into the horizon. I make my teeth the mountains and put some tall trees on either side of the road, and I add a river behind the trees on one side, flowing in the same direction as the wind. I see the leaves shaking, and some of them coming free to land on the road, and then a car comes by and runs over the leaves. I see a dragon kite with a long green tail. I see the river flowing into an ocean, and waves scrunching up into white foam, then one big wave carrying all the dead kings and queens of England and Wales and Scotland and France and Spain, smashing them on the shore, and there's a sand castle on the shore that also gets wiped out. The towers turn to wet stumps and the moat fills with salt water. Soon there's nothing, and then some man's big shoe print appears. Thinking about the ocean makes me have to pee, and I wonder if I'm allowed. Amber is sitting on the cushion next to me. I wonder if I can get away with whispering to her and asking if we can go. Probably not.

The room is warming up from all these bodies breathing.

Inside my head I see the space heater glowing in the bedroom

Bethany and I used to share. I remember a night I was lying awake in the dark, listening to the little fan in the heater. This was right before she got sick, before we knew how bad it was all going to be. I watched car lights crawling through the window, along the carpet between our beds and up the wall, sliding across our dressers. Bethany was asleep in a pocket of shadow. Her feet stuck out of the covers on the side of the bed. Her feet were all I could really see of her, when a car came by and the beams went over them like clear water, and I was kind of hypnotized by how they looked, small and perfect, like an angel's feet might look, or a fairy princess's—she'd been running around all day in a green tutu and a pair of pink and purple wings. I imagined her falling off some glittery cloud to land in our bedroom, her long hair fanned out around her face. Then she sighed and shifted, rolled over, maybe, and I couldn't see even her feet anymore. I knew she was there, though, right beyond the arc of the car lights. That's what I see now. Our old room and everything that belonged there, Bethany and me and our dressers and the lights of other people going back to their houses at night. I watch my breath fill the room, and I hold my sister inside it as long as I possibly can.

THE OTHER WOMAN

It would end in disaster, everyone said, and everyone was right, but everyone was on the outside of the situation and therefore did not know everything. She was on the inside, living with a man and in love with another woman, loving the man but not being sure anymore she should live with him, loving the extravagant Italian meals he cooked and the way he stood frowning when he painted in the corner of their living room that served as his studio, loving his longish black hair on the nape of his neck. But she also loved the longer black hair of the other woman, and how the other woman would kiss her and then pull back and look at her intently and then kiss her again, laughing; the other woman's mouth was softer than the mouth of the man she lived with, and she could not stop thinking about kissing her.

The man she lived with knew that she cared for and admired the other woman, who was older; he admired the other woman as well. She was a well-known artist represented by a prestigious gallery. So far, he had been in only a couple of inconsequential group shows, but the other woman assured him that his work would be appreciated in time. He loved his girlfriend, whom he called his partner. The other woman sometimes stayed over when they all had drunk too much, sleeping in their king-sized bed with them, and though nothing had happened between any of them (though he wasn't positive about what, exactly, had or hadn't happened on the days the two women went off alone to spend time together), he enjoyed the aura of sexual possibility. He felt as though he had two beautiful women, and when the other woman was around he felt sexier than he did with his partner, whom he had lived with for nearly six years now.

The other woman had not been with anyone for a long time, and longed for a man to be her partner. Instead, this lovely, sensual younger woman had appeared in her life to confuse and exhilarate her. Every day she listed to herself the reasons why she should not be drawn more closely into this relationship with a young couple, but in the end those reasons did not seem very important when weighed against her own loneliness. She liked the man very much; he was generous and witty, and he had promise as an artist. She was drawn to him sexually, but the younger woman had declared that she was far too jealous to share the man she lived with. The other woman thought this was wise, because things would likely fall apart very quickly if the three of them were to start up anything in bed. She thought it would be wisest not to sleep in their bed at all, but she lacked the willpower to carry through on this insight. It felt too good to lie between them, or on the side next to the wall, to occasionally feel one or the other's arms around her, to wake to the man making coffee and asking if anyone wanted toast, and if so, cream cheese, butter and jam, or just butter?

The life the young woman was living with her partner, that had once been so satisfying, had now begun to seem hollow and dull unless the other woman was around. Yet she also felt as though she was betraying her partner every time she felt this, and thought that if the other woman were not around, they might eventually return to their former domestic ease and intimacy. She tried not to call the other woman, but still she thought of her all the time, and in the end would invite her over, and feel immediately as though life was interesting again. The three of them played cards, or watched movies; they cooked meals together, or he cooked for the women while they cuddled in bed, reading to each other. On weekends, they all sometimes drove upstate for an afternoon to visit antique stores and farmer's markets. At parties they sprawled comfortably together on their hosts' couches while everyone speculated about what was going on between them. The other woman was having an affair with the man, or had become a lesbian; after years of painting men, she was now exhibiting female nudes, several of which clearly resembled the younger woman.

But the other woman had not become a lesbian and was not having an affair with anyone. It was true that the younger woman had modeled for her. But she had only kissed the younger woman, less than a handful of times. She thought she might really like the younger woman as a friend, and not a lover, but then again, life was mysterious; maybe, now that men did not seem as interested as they used to be, it was time to experiment, to explore another aspect of herself. How could she do this with the younger woman, though, without feeling as though she were betraying the friendship of the man? Even if he didn't mind—and she wasn't sure whether he would mind—she would make herself too vulnerable to the woman. Sex always made her vulnerable, and it would not be wise to give her heart to someone who also, clearly, lived with another person, slept with him every night and sorted through the bills with him and discussed who would use the car that day and who would take the train. No, it was impossible to enter into any kind of sexual affair, and she grew jealous that the younger woman had someone, while she had no one, only this halfway and increasingly unsatisfying relationship.

The man could not figure out how to make his partner happy. He would come home from work and find her crying, or in bed in the middle of the day. Lately, she didn't want to leave the house, and he often ended up having to do the grocery shopping and other errands. He was glad that she had the other woman as a friend to talk to. She called and texted the other woman every day. Whenever she talked to the other woman, her voice grew light, and happy, and he felt this was a good sign, and that soon she would shake off whatever was bothering her.

Then the other woman had a show in England and went away for several weeks. The man's partner grew more and more withdrawn, and often seemed angry at him. She was never in the mood to make love. He worried now that she would fall into the kind of terrible depression she had suffered around the time they had first met, when he had been married, when the woman who was now his partner had been the other woman.

What a mess that had been. Disaster, in the end. Eventually that time had begun to feel like the distant past, as though those miserable, confusing events had happened to other people. All that was over, finished.

Although lately, certain memories of his ex-wife had resurfaced. How she had woken him one morning by putting her mouth on him. How she would laugh after accidentally burning dinner, or spilling wine on their new sheets, but be upset at mishearing something he said. The times she had slammed a door on him, only to immediately, contritely, open it again. The images struck him with surprising clarity and immediacy. At night he lay in bed with his partner, filled with those images, painful reminders that in spite of his deep love for his wife, and his best intentions, he had failed to keep his promises to her; when his partner rolled over in sleep and moved against him, he turned away.

NIGHT OWLS

Sometimes I like to take off from campus and go downtown to the fancy hotels, where they have piano music and the bartenders wear tuxes. I order a Lemon Drop and read Charlotte Brontë or Jane Austen in the muted bar light, wearing a tasteful black dress, my hair piled demurely on my head, little ringlets escaping down my neck. I wait for a man to come over, which never takes long. But when I get upstairs, into a room with him, I change completely. I order him to take his clothes off, to lie down on the bed and close his eyes. They always smile like crazy at that point, they can't believe their luck. I tell him I'm going to make him feel good, and I can see he's thinking about how he'll tell the story the next day to his best friend at work, about meeting this girl in the hotel bar. I put my hand on him through his briefs or boxers and remind him to keep his eyes closed. I take out my lace handkerchief, and the chloroform, and before he knows what's happening he's passed out and I'm straddling him, my fangs in his neck, his blood pouring down my throat.

The men I meet downtown are perfect: married, a little drunk, a little overweight. It's bad if they're thin, because by the time I have my fill they're practically comatose. I don't want to kill them, just feed on them enough to keep me going. If I were a full vampire it might be different, but I'm only half, on my dad's side. My dad has to kill people to get enough. I understand, I guess, but I don't like to think about it, and I'm happy I never killed anyone. Even the coma thing only happened once.

So tonight I'm sitting in a fancy bar off the lobby of the Marriott with my Lemon Drop, reading Edith Wharton. It's *The House of Mirth,* for English Lit. Lily Bart has just blown her chance to marry the rich but boring Percy Gryce. She's supposed to meet him to go to church, but instead she sneaks off with this guy Selden and sits on a bench in the woods with him. It's early in the novel, but I can already tell that she's not going to end up with Selden. She likes money too much, and while her heart is with Selden it's pretty clear he won't be able to afford her. Lily's a creature of comfort, and she can't change. She has to have expensive gowns and lavish dinner parties and Mediterranean vacations. I put the book down on the bar, thinking how sad it is that people can't just follow their hearts.

That's when I notice the guy sitting at the table by the fireplace, watching me. He's big and muscular and handsome, his eyes dark as an oil spill. My mouth goes dry and I feel hunger like a scalpel turning and twisting inside me, making my stomach cramp. I stare at the veins in his thick neck. He looks like a body builder and I wonder if I'll have a problem putting him down. Sometimes, figuring out the dose can be tricky. "Leave the big ones alone," my dad used to say. "I worry about you," he said, "on your own in a city so far away. Stick to small animals. You can survive on animal blood." He doesn't know I graduated from dogs and cats, from squirrels and pigeons and chickens, when I discovered how good boys tasted. That was right after I discovered that my dad didn't stick to animals, either. One night in my senior year of high school I ran into him. I was coming out of a club, kind of drunk, and there he was in the alley, crouched over a girl. I backed up into the doorway and watched him feeding on her until she lay there drained of life, a sprawled thing in a green dress not much older than I was. We got in a big fight about it. The next night I went out and fed on my first boy and put him in the ICU for six months.

I study the guy, trying to calculate the dose, and because I've had more to drink than I should and am feeling reckless, I decide it's worth a try. He doesn't come over, just looks at me, and finally I pick up my napkin and drink and book and walk over to him.

"Mind if I join you?" I say.

"For what, honey?" he says, and smirks a little. He runs a hand through his hair and I see it's ever-so-slightly thinning on top.

"A drink. Some conversation. Some company."

"Are you old enough for that?" he says, indicating my Lemon Drop.

"Sure," I lie. I'm nineteen, but my ID says twenty-three.

He looks around quickly and then says, in a low voice, "How much?" He stares at my breasts, like he knows what they look like under my clothes.

"You think I'm a hooker?" I say, kind of loud. Like I said, I've had a little too much to drink.

He looks around again, freaked out now. "Hey," he says. "Hey. Keep your voice down."

"You've got it all wrong. I don't sleep with guys for money."

"Okay," he says. "I've got it all wrong." He's drinking Evian. Maybe he's in training for something. I imagine him naked on the sheets of one of the hotel's king beds, a fat-marbled slab of steak on a white platter, dripping with juice.

"I forgive you." I set down my drink, slip *The House of Mirth* into my purse, and pull up the heavy upholstered chair. "I'm Tiffany." Of course I'm not going to tell him my real name. My dad named me Bogdana, which is some weird Slavic name. My mom shortened it to Dana, and that's what I've always gone by. A solid, normal American name.

"Tiffany," he says. "A beautiful name for a beautiful girl."

"Thank you." I give him a tiny smile. I can feel my fangs aching, wanting to come through my gums. In another minute they will, that's how hungry I am.

He goes back to staring at my breasts. "Does that mean you sleep with guys for no money?" he says. "Because you really are a very sexy girl."

"Why thank you, sir," I say, giving it the Southern drawl I've been practicing.

"Sorry we got off on the wrong page there," he says. "Page, get it? You were reading a book." Like he's the cleverest thing in the world. Stupid pig.

I smile at him, slip my stockinged foot out of its high heel, and bring it up to rub the inside of his thigh.

. . .

There's a boy I like at school, but he's got a girlfriend already. His name used to be Lawrence, but he changed it to Leo his first semester, because he thinks it's cooler. The Theater majors are divided into the ones who really do want to be theater actors, like me, and the ones who wanted to head straight to Hollywood after high school but got told by their parents that they'd better go to college or they'd be cut off financially. Those are the ones who change their names freshman year, figuring they'll have a better chance when they graduate and end up in a major motion picture. They think their unique, special qualities will shine brighter than anybody else's, that they'll be lounging around their pool in Beverly Hills between phone calls from Martin Scorcese and the Coen brothers. They practice being interviewed by that guy on the Actor's Studio who asks things like, "What is your favorite curse word?" and "What sound or noise do you love?" when what they should be practicing is something else entirely, like "My name is Leo and I'll be your waitperson."

Leo is beautiful enough to hold his own in Hollywood if he ever ends up there. When he took off his shirt after yoga class yesterday, I couldn't stop staring at his nipples. That's usually not the kind of thing that turns me on, but looking at his pale, muscled chest, the few little black hairs right in the center, and then his nipples all puckered up in the cold of the studio—I even made a little sound in my throat, that his girl-friend, Roxie, heard; she cut her eyes at me and walked right over to him, checking herself out in the mirrors as she went, and gave him a big kiss. Which he hated, I know. Leo does not like Public Displays of Affection.

Talk about a drama queen: Roxie sweeps around in long black capes and boots with flame decals on them, and wears short tight dresses even now, in February, when it's about a zillion degrees below zero. Roxie hates me because I'm friends with Leo, and she knows I want it to be more, but she can't stop me from seeing him. Leo and I go to Pizza Hut for the pepperoni special, and to the midnight movie downtown, or we hang around in his dorm room because his roommate is never there, unlike mine, who scurries to class and the cafeteria and comes straight back to study and cry about her pathetic life. Leo tells Roxie she has nothing to worry about, but she hates me anyway. She's not stupid; she senses something. After kissing Leo at yoga class she waited until he changed his shirt and left, and then she came over to me, acting like she wanted to be my friend.

"Hey, sweetie," she said. Everybody in the program says that, but when Roxie says it, it sounds so fake. "Want to hang out Sunday night?" She knew Leo and I had plans to memorize our lines for *The Glass Menagerie* that night. "Oh, right," she said, as if suddenly remembering that fact. "You'll be with my man."

I wanted to choke her.

"I know what you're up to, Dana. Don't think I won't fight for him."

"I don't want to fight you," I said.

"Good. Because you'd lose." She looked at herself in the mirror behind my head and flipped back her dyed black hair.

64

I thought of my dad, who doesn't even show up in mirrors—there's just a kind of tarnish that appears, like someone has leaned close and exhaled a black mist of breath. I knew I was there in the mirror, though, and I wished I wasn't. It felt like being caught, pinned down.

"I know you want him," Roxie said, studying herself, not even looking at me now. Like I was so far beneath her she didn't need to bother. "Watch out, I'm on to you," she said, then walked away, leaving me to gather up my stuff.

I do want Leo. I want to be with him in total darkness, without any light coming in under the door of his dorm room. I want to feel his tongue slide over my incisors, to breathe in his smell of Marlboros and sweat and Calvin Klein One, and feed on him—but gently, just sucking on his neck, giving him a common, ordinary hickey. I want him to understand how hard it is to pretend all the time that I'm just like everybody else. I think he might be able to understand, if I explained it to him in the right way, because we talked a lot, when we both took Personal Identity, about Nature and Nurture. My dad tells me that my mom understands him, and that's why they get along, why they've been married for so long. *Honesty and communication*, my dad always says. *That's the ticket.*

. . .

Even though it's after two a.m. when I get back from the hotel—not to mention the fact that it's a Saturday night—my roommate, Sharon, is up studying for her Abnormal Psych exam. My roommate is a clueless wonder who, when she wants to move her desk an inch or put up a picture torn out from a cat calendar, comes to me and says things like, "Dana, I'm being proactive here." Then she asks my permission. She claims she was date-raped last semester by one of her professors, which I don't believe for a minute, especially since she also goes around telling everybody she's a virgin. She wrote a song about the date rape thing and recorded it on a CD to help her through her trauma. She plays it day and night, and rocks back and forth kneeling on her bed, her long frizzy red hair swinging across her face. Pathetic girls like her are always Psych majors. If a girl like Sharon can get a college degree and hang out a therapist's shingle, it kind of makes you wonder.

When I walk in, the CD of her song is playing softly on her boom box. She got somebody to accompany her on guitar, and I hate to say it, but she doesn't sound half bad. The song is called "Sordid Sex," and I swear it could be a hit on one of those Christian rock stations, because it's all about how the girl wants a meaningful relationship and the guy just wants to get laid. The best part comes in the middle, though, when the guitar stops and Sharon starts talking. That's the part I walk in on.

"Okay, boys and girls," she says, in a game show host kind of voice. "Let's get out our Ken and Barbie date rape dolls! Barbie says, I'm drawing a clear boundary here: no sex. Ken says,"—and here Sharon's voice drops down a register, getting kind of spooky and hollow—"I feel *closer* to a woman when I have sex." Then it's back to Barbie. "Barbie says, I said no sex." But then Ken asks if he can just give her a massage. It goes on a little longer while I peel off my dress, feeling relaxed and woozy from the body builder's blood; he tasted even better than he looked, thick and syrupy. Ken keeps trying to talk Barbie into it, rubbing her neck and shoulders, telling her she talks too much, that she should just let go. Ken employs some empathy, Sharon explains, and then Barbie panics. After Sharon says "panics" there's a moment of total silence. Then the guitar starts up again, three driving chords, and it's back to the chorus. There's a good line, too, that goes, "What is consensual sex," but the way Sharon sings it she lands hard on the "con" so it sounds like "cunt." Overall it's a pretty catchy song, but I'm sick of it by now.

"Sharon," I say. "Are you going to play that all night?"

"Sorry." She drops her head, hiding behind her hair. She acts scared of me, I don't know why. Maybe somebody told her that I played her song for all my friends when she was at class, and that we've acted out Barbie's date rape, laughing hysterically. Theater students will act out anything at the drop of a hat.

Sharon turns off her boom box. There's a sticker on the side of it that says, *You Deserve To Be Loved.* "Is the light going to bother you, Dana?" she asks. "I can turn it off. Even though I'm not done studying."

Victim, I think. *Passive-aggressive little bitch.*

"No problem," I tell her. "Leave it on. I'm up."

Artificial light, I'm fine with. Daylight I can sort of handle, as long as I wear heavy sunscreen, but it makes my skin itch if I'm out too long. My dad, of course, stays inside all day, sleeping in the basement of the house I grew up in and still go back to in the summers and at Christmas. Daylight makes my dad deathly ill. My mom, though, loves to lie on a chaise lounge out on the deck, or on a blanket on the beach, slathered with cocoa butter.

She's kind of a sun worshipper, my mom.

.   .   .

Sunday night Leo and I are dancing in his dorm room, between his bed and his desk, practicing the scene from *The Glass Menagerie* where Jim and Laura waltz around, bump into the table full of Laura's glass animals, and break the unicorn. We don't know how to waltz so we're faking it, turning in small circles, my hand on Leo's shoulder. Leo has his hand lightly on my hip and I want someone to come along and weld it there.

He laughs, *Ha-ha-ha*, then kind of pushes me against his roommate's desk and lets his hand drop.

"What did we hit on?" he says, as Jim.

"Table," I say, giving the "a" a bit of my Southern accent. We go through the next part, Laura acting like she's not devastated over having the horn knocked off her treasured unicorn. Next Jim gives a sexy little pep talk to Laura, setting her up before he crushes her with the news of his great love for Betty.

"Ha-ha, that's very funny!" Leo says in his Jim accent. "I'm glad to see that you have a sense of humor. You know—you're—well—very different! Surprisingly different from anyone else I know!"

We move to his bed and sit down, side by side, going back on book because neither of us has memorized the next part yet. He goes on telling me how pretty I am, calling me Blue Roses. I let myself be Laura, naïve and trusting. I imagine blue roses blooming all over my body, thinking maybe I'll get a tattoo.

"Somebody ought to—ought to—*kiss* you, Laura!" Leo says.

"*His hand slips slowly up her arm to her shoulder,*" I say, reading the stage directions. "*Music swells tumultuously.*" I wait for Leo to touch me, but he doesn't. "*He suddenly turns her about and kisses her on the lips,*" I read, but Leo doesn't move, so I just keep reading until it's his turn to say "Stumble-john!" about his clumsy self. He says it a few times while he weasels his way out of seeing poor crippled Laura ever again.

I take his hand and gently put a pack of Marlboros in his palm, a stand-in for the broken unicorn Laura gives Jim. I close his fingers around it, bite my lip, and say, "A—souvenir…"

That's the end of our scene, before Laura's mother, Amanda, comes in with fruit punch and macaroons.

"Wow," Leo says. "Nice job. I need a cigarette. Take a walk?"

He's already off the bed, sticking the cigarettes in his back pocket. Stay, I want to say. That's what Roxie would do. She orders him around all the time. Of course I don't say anything, because, as my dad says, if you care for something you have to let it go and wait for it to come back to you. So I just follow Leo down the hall to the elevator.

We head over to the strip of shops and bars and cafés where everybody from school hangs out, but we don't go in anywhere even though it's freezing. We walk until we get to the museum a few blocks away and wander around among the statues in the sculpture garden. Then we sit on a cold cement bench in front of an abstract angel with big metal wings that revolve slowly in the wind. Leo rummages in his backpack and brings out a package of Pepperidge Farm cheddar goldfish crackers, which he knows are my favorite. Leo is thoughtful like that. We pass the bag back and forth.

"It's so sad," Leo says. "She has wings, but she just goes around and around. Wouldn't it be cool if she could just fly off?"

"Expatiate," I say.

"Meaning what?"

"To roam, to wander freely." It's a word I learned from my dad. He's big on expanding your vocabulary. When I was little, he'd read to me from the dictionary, explaining the Greek and Latin derivations of the words, talking wistfully about ancient times, when, he said, the world was a more civilized place. He's got a streak of nostalgia a mile wide. When I go home this Christmas he'll probably drag out the videos, as usual, and cry over me as a baby in diapers, a five-year-old biting into a hamster (my mom will head for the kitchen when that one comes on), a gawky preadolescent opening presents under the tree in new silk pajamas. Then he'll expatiate all night, looking for some girl coming home late from a party. He'll swoop down on her and drag her into the bushes, while my mom turns off the tree lights and gets into bed alone.

"I love that you know so many words," Leo says. "You're so smart."

He puts his arm around me for a second, just to give me a friendly squeeze. I think of what he just said. *Love. You. So.*

"Let's fly," Leo says. He pulls me up and starts twirling me around, faster and faster, until I shriek for him to stop. My feet lift off the ground, but he's strong enough to hold me like that, parallel to the frosted grass, spinning. Then he staggers back and falls, and I land on top of him. I think that's the exact minute—feeling his body beneath mine, my breasts against his chest, the sharpness of the cold air in my lungs—that I feel this kind of lurch in my heart that tells me I more than like him. He strokes my hair, and then his hand moves, once, down along my body before he suddenly rolls from under me and sits up.

"Dana, I'm sorry," he says.

"Don't be. Please." The angel's wings go creak, creak, creak. She needs to be oiled, I guess.

"I care about you so much," Leo says. "You're not just some girl to me."

I want to tell him right then. I want to blurt everything out, about how much I feel for him, about who I really am, but then I'm afraid he'll think I'm weird and won't like me anymore.

"I think I kind of, you know," Leo says.

"What?" I say.

He leans in and hugs me, hard.

"Don't say kind of," I say, my face squashed against his shoulder.

• • •

"How's school?" my mom says on the phone. "Do you like your classes?"

"I'm getting all As. I'm kind of stressed, though. We're doing a play. I have classes all day, and then rehearsals until ten-thirty p.m."

"I hope you're getting enough sleep at night."

71

"You know me. I don't need much sleep."

"A night owl, like your father," she says.

My mom knows what my dad is, but she mostly acts like she doesn't. She knows he's going to live forever, looking exactly like he does now, and she's going to get old and wrinkled from the sun and die one day. She knows he's been married several times before, that he feeds on blood but would never harm a hair on her head. I don't think she knows about the girls. She told me once that she had asked my father to suck her blood, just a little, and he refused. But usually she's not that direct. She says my father is different, that I take after him in some ways, but in other ways I'm more like her.

"You need to take it easy," she says. "You're so hard on yourself."

Virginal date-raped Sharon is sitting on her bed, watching me pace back and forth in our room. I'm trying to find a place my cell phone won't cut out. I move as far away from her as I can.

"Where's Daddy? Is he home?"

"Oh, you know your father. Out roaming around somewhere or other. He said to tell you he forgot to send your allowance but he finally mailed it today."

"Is that it? That's the only message?"

"Just the usual," my mom says. "He loves you. Be careful."

"I *am* careful."

"Dana, honey—"

"What?"

"Are you getting enough to eat?"

"I'm fine, Mom. Trust me. I'm all right."

When I click off my phone I feel like gorging on something salty—pretzel rings, Doritos, fried tofu in soy sauce. I feel like going over to the indoor track and dragging off a runner in his sweaty warm-ups.

"What is it?" Sharon says. She's still watching me. I mean, get a life. Once I caught her smelling my blue turtleneck sweater, just sitting on her bed holding it in her lap, hunched over with her face buried in it. "You look sad," she says. "Do you want to share anything?"

"No, Sharon, I don't want to *share*. And I don't want any healing sage or crystals, either, or any transpersonal Gestalt Freudian bullshit psychobabble. Just leave me the fuck alone."

She picks up her iPod and lies down on her bed and clamps her earphones on, and I know what she's listening to. She's such a fucking freak I can't believe it.

• • •

I've been feeding more often lately. I seem to need more and more just to feel normal, to get a couple of hours of sleep before classes and rehearsals start. I'm tired and sluggish, and I'm falling asleep in my nine a.m. class—Gender and Sexual Politics in America—which I'm usually wide awake for, since I've been thinking about minoring in American Studies.

I go farther out, taking buses into the neighboring towns, afraid of running into someone who might recognize me. I try not to hit the same place twice, except for the hotels, where I figure the clientele changes pretty frequently. This week I had a taste of a PhD student whose thesis is on somebody named Lacan. I had a black performance artist from a wealthy suburb whose work, he said, was "all about how I've been battling terrorism since I was a baby," and a District Sales Manager for Pepsi who was drinking rum-and-Cokes and looking around furtively, like he was being watched by the Pepsi Gestapo. Nobody who didn't deserve it. I picked them for their shallowness, their stupidity, the way they talked about women.

And tonight. Tonight I'm over at the junior high, practicing a trick my dad showed me, that I'm still trying to master. I turn into a bat and flap up along the icy bleachers on the dark field, at the end next to the scoreboard. There are still numbers up from the last game. Wolverines 21, Badgers 10. At first I can only go up a few rows, but after a couple of hours of practice I can reach the top row before changing back. Finally I fly off the bleachers and cruise around a little, kind of slow and wobbly, back and forth above the field, and while I'm up there I catch sight of a boy in the parking lot at the far end, unlocking a bicycle from a metal rack. He's having trouble because he's wearing thick gloves. Finally he takes off the gloves, sets them next to the bike, and undoes the lock. While he's leaning over, I swoop down on him. I force him onto the asphalt and drink the liquid candy-and-chocolate-milk taste of him. I feel famished, even though I fed a few hours ago, and maybe I overdo it a little. When I finally get up off him, he looks pretty bad.

I walk back holding my stomach, which is churning like I ate some greasy Chinese takeout from the place only clueless freshmen go to. The streets are empty, the bars already closed, the red neon martini glass of the one closest to campus gone

74

gray and dull. The dorm halls are lit up and sad. I go straight to the bathroom on our floor, into a stall, and puke. I look at the blood spreading out into the water in the toilet bowl and think I might be losing it.

· · ·

"What's wrong?" Leo says. "You sick or something?"

We're in his room, lying on our stomachs reading the script, close together on his long narrow bed. Our shoulders are touching, and I'm inhaling his breath, Altoid mints and underneath that salty McDonald's french fries, and saliva, and under that, I'm sure, there's a faint heady mineral trace. Leo's blood.

"Nothing. I'm fine."

"You don't look fine," Leo says, nudging my shoulder with his, a short, sharp push.

I give him a shove back.

"Quit it," I say.

"You," he says, leaning his whole body into me, and before we know it we're wrestling and laughing, and I'm tickling his waist and armpits, and then he's got me pinned underneath him, his body stretched over mine, our pelvises fitting perfectly together. We stop moving and just lie there, both of us breathing fast. My ear is against his chest and I can feel his heart beating hard; I can feel mine, too, only mine is more fluttery, like something knocking around a room it's flown into.

"Leo," I say. "I don't like myself very much right now." The boy at the junior high made the newspaper. *Mysterious illness,* the article said. The word *vampire* wasn't mentioned. Still, my dad would kill me if he knew what I've been up to.

"Forget about her." Leo thinks I feel bad about Roxie. "I like *you*," he says.

"You don't know me," I say.

"Shh." He starts to move against me, and it's like our clothes aren't even there. I feel heavy, and liquid, like a river full of mud and debris. I'm sinuous and undulating and moving like a river, down a hillside, entering a deep canyon. Up above me there's a shape, silhouetted black against the sun.

"No," I say. "No. I don't want to."

Leo rolls away immediately. He gets off the bed and goes to stand in the corner of the room, like it's a timeout in grade school.

"I'm sorry," he says. "Shit. I'm sorry. I didn't mean to do anything, if you didn't want to."

"Just leave me alone from now on. I don't think of you like that."

"We're still friends, aren't we? Don't say we can't be friends." He slumps back against the wall. "Blue Roses," he says.

"Blue is wrong for roses," I say, which is the next line of the play, but I don't say it like Laura would. I say it like Roxie might—Roxie, who is a terrible actress, who never gets the tone, the intention of the line. I say it nastily, the way someone would say, *You haven't got a fucking clue*, and then I walk out past him and slam the door so hard I can hear his roommate's dart board fall off the wall behind me.

The next day we have to do the scene in front of everybody. Everybody includes Roxie, slumped in the front row with her arms crossed and her legs stuck straight out in front of her. She knows we're supposed to kiss, and she's giving me a look that says, *If you put your tongue in his mouth I will kill you.*

Leo and I *cut the rug* a little, like the play says. When we get to the kissing part he slides his hand up my shoulder, fast, like he wants to get it over with, and then leans in. His lips are soft as clouds. He doesn't mash them into me, like some boys would, just puts them there for me to touch. I brush them gently, and then it's over and we go on to the end of the scene, when I open my hand to give him the unicorn. It's a little ceramic horse I stole from Sharon, and I can't keep my hand from shaking.

. . .

I swear off blood for a week. I drink a lot of Snapple Lemonade, for the sugar. Every morning I take a half-dozen iron pills, washing them down with can after can of thick red V-8. I can't avoid Leo at rehearsals, but afterwards I rush out of the black box theater, and Roxie is always right there to pounce on him and keep him from me. I hang with the friends I'd been ignoring in order to spend so much time with Leo. One night we go to the bar across town that has bowling lanes, and I get drunk on raspberry vodka and heave ball after heavy, swirly ball at the helpless pins. I try to crawl under the machine that sets up the pins, and get knocked on the back of the head by the steel bar swinging down, and the owner very nicely tells us all to leave. My friends can see something's up and pretty much figure it out, but when they bring up Leo's name I say, "New topic," and that's that.

Except I miss him. I miss him reciting the Kevin Costner speech from *Bull Durham* about what Crash believes in, and Dennis Hopper's crazy rap from *Apocalypse Now*. I miss watching him smoke a cigarette, scraping it along a brick wall when he's done and putting it in his pocket or a trash can instead of tossing the butt on the street the way other guys would. I call his cell phone when I know he's in class to hear his recorded message—his prison guard voice from *Cool Hand Luke*, saying, "What we got here is a f-failure to communicate." Then, in his Leo voice, he says, "Leave a message," and I hang up.

This kind of agony is normal. All my girlfriends say so. They've been there, they say, and even though I say, "New topic," and hold my ears, I hear them, I know. Love sucks.

. . .

The backstage dressing room is ugly, ringed with yellow bulbs and ripply mirrors, the floor scarred by the shoes and slippers of a thousand aspiring actors. Everyone's joking and giggling, having a last cigarette or fussing over their stage makeup. It's the dress rehearsal, so things feel more real than when we were wearing our regular clothes. I put on the dorky dress that makes me Laura, pull my hair back with a white ribbon, and work on numbing myself in the face of impending proximity to Leo. Our director sits on a chair turned backwards, flirting with the girl who plays Amanda, Laura's mother. He's got a wife and baby in his other life, but every semester he looks for a female student willing to date him. There's always one. It's always over at the end of the semester. He thinks nobody knows, but everybody laughs about him behind his back, except the one.

Leo has been drinking. I smell it on him as soon as he walks onstage, offering me his hand. He flubs a few lines, but we all just keep going. He's definitely drunk by the last scene; we don't have to fake falling into the table with the little glass animals. It all feels like it takes forever, and by the time I blow the candles out, ending the play, I'm wiped out. I don't bother taking off my dress—the new, prettier one I'm wearing by then—just stuff my jeans and sweater into my backpack and throw on my coat. I go down the halls and the echoing stairs and cut across the big open lawn toward my dorm.

"Wait, wait," Leo calls. He catches up to me by the duck pond. I don't know why they call it that because there are never any ducks. It's just a little oval of slimy water, surrounded by some trees.

"We need to talk," he says.

"I don't think so." I stop under a tree and lean my forehead against it.

"I brought some raspberry vodka to tempt you." He sits on the grass, pulling it from his backpack. "Have some," he says.

I guess he's holding out the bottle, but I don't know, because I've closed my eyes. I like how the tree smells, like bark and rot.

"Please, Dana. I can't stand this anymore."

I go over and take the bottle and chug some, and immediately feel kind of drunk. Though not any better.

"My turn," he says, and he goes ahead and chugs it, too. "Hey, Blue Roses," he says, but it comes out "Blue Roshes."

We hand the bottle back and forth, not talking. Across the lawn, some of the rooms in the dorms are lit, people up late studying or partying. Music from different stereos mixes in the air, tangled threads of bass thumps and guitar chords. Sharon's probably playing her song, and I'm glad I can't hear it. I can hear the techs who did the lighting for the rehearsal, just leaving the theater building. They're laughing hysterically, going "No way, dude" and "Way" to each other, walking away from campus toward town. There's nobody else around, and we're kind of hidden, over by the trees in the dark, and I feel really alone.

"I shouldn't have tried anything," Leo says finally.

"Is that what Roxie says?" I say, shivering under my coat.

"I went and ruined our friendship."

"Whatever," I say, like I couldn't care less.

He takes another big swig from the bottle, for courage I guess, and puts his arm around me.

"Forgive me," he says, putting his head on my shoulder. "Be my friend."

I turn and burrow into him. He holds me for a minute, and then I push him back, and lie on top of him, opening my coat to cover us both.

"Leo," I say.

He lets his head fall a little to the side and closes his eyes. He rolls his head back and forth. "Darling Dana," he says dreamily.

And then, well. He's right there. And I'm so hungry. One snarl, and I've got him by the neck.

"Stop it," he says, over and over.

But I can't. It's like I've been waiting for this particular flavor my whole life, without even knowing it. He's fighting me, bucking beneath me and trying to throw me off. But

I've got him gripped tightly, and he's had way more to drink than I have. With every swallow of him I feel stronger, more alive, while he gets more disoriented, until he's limp beneath me.

I stop for a minute, raising my face above his, looking into his beautiful brown eyes.

"This is who I am," I tell him. "This is who I really am." My mouth is full of his blood. I can feel it dripping down my chin like hot melted ice cream.

The way he looks at me then is terrible.

. . .

My dad and I have a heart-to-heart, after the thing with Leo, after I drop out of college. He says you can't let them get to you, that they're just food. He says when I meet someone really special, it will be different, and that's the one I should marry. He said he knew right away, with my mother, that he could never touch her that way. And maybe I'll get lucky and find one of our own kind.

"Sometimes," he says, "I think I shouldn't have married your mother. But then I wouldn't have you."

We're in the den, and I'm curled up on his lap on the couch, the way I sometimes used to do when I was younger. He'd come into my room at night and carry me out to watch TV with him, and let me stay up until gray light came in through the cracks of the heavy curtains that cover the sliding glass doors. My mother always made me go to bed at a normal hour, but I'd be wide awake in the middle of the night, talking to my dolls or just lying there thinking about how amazing it would be to fly and walk through walls and be invisible. And it will be. It will be amazing. I'll fly high above them, and swoop down just long enough, and be gone before they ever knew what hit them.

"I loved him, Daddy," I say. "I loved him, and I killed him."

"Such a sensitive child," he says, stroking my hair. Then he smiles, showing his fangs.

THE PALACE OF ILLUSIONS

That summer I was twenty-one. I worked in a big tent with the words *The Palace of Illusions* in blue on a white banner stretched across the entrance, making doves vanish from cages, holding a big snake by the neck so it would coil around my chest, sawing my girlfriend, Alice, in half inside a box or cutting off her head. When she talked, a seemingly disembodied head on a platform across the room from the rest of her, girls would scream and sometimes faint in their boyfriends' arms. I liked to think it was my skills, not just the sultry weather and the beer everyone was guzzling from wide plastic cups. I was the Illusionist. I made believers out of skeptics, convinced ordinary people of an extraordinary world that existed just on my stage. I was good, is what I'm saying.

I bet you were, the girl said. This is your studio?

She was taking in my room, the water-stained wallpaper with the roses on it, the frayed edge of the carpet. My hot plate on top of the waist-high refrigerator. Cans of spaghetti and soup, neatly stacked next to the sink. For real? she said.

Here, you can check out some of my work, I said. I took my photo album off the dresser. The cover is white leather, with gold bells stamped on it. Inside, couples feed each other cake and kiss. It makes a nice presentation.

She still had half a slice of the pizza I'd bought her on the boardwalk. She set it carefully on the refrigerator in the wax paper, wiped her hands on her short skirt, and took the album.

These are nice, she said after a minute. Everybody looks so happy.

Thanks. You can just sit on the bed.

She sat, crossing her legs, balancing the album on one thigh. She had a bruise there about the size of a sand dollar, yellowed and nearly gone. You almost couldn't notice it. I wondered if it would show up in the photos.

I've never done this before, she said.

It's not hard, I said. You just need to sit there. Or you can lie down, if you want. Realistic is good. I screwed the camera onto the tripod, which I keep set up in the corner by the dresser, and looked through the lens. If you just want to take off your shirt and bra, that's fine, I said. I can pay you more for full nudity though.

Okay. She put the album on the floor and set her blue nylon backpack on top of it. She stood up and pulled her T-shirt over her head, then stepped out of her heels and unzipped her skirt. She removed her bra, and her panties that had a kitty's face on them, and stood there pressing her legs together.

Why don't you put the heels back on, I said. It usually makes for a better picture.

She slipped them on again, and her naked legs looked longer.

She was tiny, like Holly was. Was, because Holly's dead now. Deader than a doornail, as Don John said earlier on the phone, giving me the news. The phone's down the hall. It never rings for me, but this time it did.

Doornail, Don John repeated. Ha ha, he said, and then coughed. I didn't mean it like that, he said. In the carnival, Don John used to do a blockhead act, putting a five-inch spike up his nose.

A friend of mine just died, I told the girl.

I'm sorry, the girl said, sitting back down on the bed. What was her name?

Holly, I said. I hadn't said her name aloud in years.

What was she like?

Long story, I said.

• • •

The train was rocking along at a pretty good clip, somewhere between Hutchinson, Kansas, and Ardmore, Oklahoma, which was our carnival's next stop. Outside the windows, the dull world barely registered before it was gone: backyards where clothes flapped empty on lines, overturned tricycles, seas of rusted stripped cars next to tire mountains, gas stations, broken-windowed factories. It was ugly and ordinary, like the town in Ohio where I grew up, and I was glad not to be a part of it anymore. My mother had left me and my dad when I was nine, and my dad was an alcoholic who smacked me around before I was big enough to defend myself. When I got older he left me alone, except to steal money from me. I lived with him while I went to the state university because I couldn't afford a place of my own. When I got my degree I looked around for anything that would get me out of town.

Alice was lying on her berth, looking like she was asleep, and I picked up my camera. She was the first girl I'd ever made love to, and even though I'd seen her naked, she was still as new to me as the freaks and cons we were traveling with. Alice and I had joined the carnival together. She'd been my girlfriend for six months. Now she was the Illusionist's Beautiful Assistant. Put your hands together and welcome her, ladies and gentlemen. I'd brought my Nikon and a duffel bag of Tri-X, planning to make a portfolio that would land me a scholarship to art school somewhere. Somehow I had managed to talk sensible, pre-med-in-the-fall Alice into a little pink outfit and cape and high heels. Besides my interest in getting close to what was under her clothing and possibly swirling inside her level head, I was afraid I'd be lonely without a companion. I knew I could handle the act— I'd been doing magic since high school—but I didn't know about traveling alone with a bunch of carnies. So it was a relief when she'd shrugged and said, Sure, Martin, I'll do it, and started organizing the clothes on the floor of my closet so I could decide what to bring.

I didn't try to hold the camera steady, figuring it might be interesting to see how the motion of the train blurred her face. She was dreaming, I thought from the twitching of her closed lids, and I wished there were a camera that could capture what went on inside her head so I could study her dreams later, in private. My own dreams were filled with carnies. Darryl the Gentle Giant in his size 22 shoes. Missy Mister, the half-man, half-woman. Lobster Girl with her deformed hands. Don John, who ran the Scrambler and ate fire and also did the blockhead act. In my dreams, the carnival had set up its tents and rides, and I wondered if that was the case with Alice.

Martin, Alice said, surprising me. Her eyes were still closed. I don't want you to take my picture, okay?

I thought you were sleeping.

I was.

I popped off one more, just to annoy her. It was a bad habit I'd fallen into over the last couple of weeks—annoying Alice. We'd been together constantly for almost a month, fighting over things like my leaving the toothpaste uncapped or losing the sunglasses she kept replacing for me in every town. Lately, even when she was right next to me, I felt like she was miles away. If she got mad enough, she'd come back from wherever she was and talk to me.

Outside the compartment, Holly went by, singing "A Hundred Bottles of Beer on the Wall." Everybody passed our compartment on the way from the poker game to the bathrooms at the end of the car.

I lowered my camera and set it in my open suitcase on the floor, on top of my jumbled T-shirts. Alice rolled over in her narrow berth, turning her back to me. One strap of her halter slid down her shoulder, revealing a pale white strip that had been hidden from the sun, and I picked up the camera again.

There goes Holly, Alice said to the wall.

Let's smoke some pot, I said.

Pass, Alice said.

I rummaged through the junk on the narrow corner shelf

and found my marble pipe and the baggie. I guess she and Jack had a fight, I said.

She's such a—Alice turned toward me, looking for the right word. She would never say *bitch*, but I thought that was probably the word she wanted. There were a few I might have used, like *sexy* and even *glamorous*, but not in front of Alice. You know, she said, turning over and watching me, it's probably not good to alter your brain chemistry so often.

Do you think they had a fight? I said.

THC causes convulsions in rats, she said. Alice had already bought some of the textbooks for her classes. She had been telling me all week about animal experiments. Rats, for example, sometimes were forced to swim until they drowned. Alice hardly ever smoked pot.

She coughed when I lit the match, like the smoke was already getting to her. Last night, she said, Holly was yelling at Jack in front of their trailer, telling him he was bad in bed. She said she'd rather you-know-what a monkey. The word had probably never passed Alice's lips.

Pretty harsh, I said, taking a hit. Holly and Jack, the carnival's owner, usually traveled separately from the rest of us in an Airstream trailer. I thought of Holly standing in front of Jack in her tight capri pants, her overdone makeup, her white-blonde hair teased up. Telling him off, though he was twice her size. She wasn't a midget, but she was small—a tiny woman with enormous breasts that always looked, when they swerved your way, like they were being offered on a platter. She had a voice as sharp as the spikes on her high heels. Alice and I hadn't been able to stop talking about her since first being introduced. Holly was a second assistant for some of the tricks in my act, when she wasn't too drunk.

Alice said, I'd never talk to you the way she talks to Jack, if we were married. Poor guy. Holly's on him all the time.

Yeah, I said. I looked around for my camera, realizing I'd set it down at some point. The pot was really good sensimilla. I'd bought it from Dani, a female midget chanteuse who dressed in feather boas and sequined cocktail dresses. I flashed on Holly in bed, riding Jack's big stomach, her breasts bobbing and swaying, and I began to get hard. Alice and I hadn't made love since Calgary, several stops ago.

Do you think we should get married someday? Alice said.

She had propped herself up on an elbow and was watching me, like she was seriously considering it. I held the pot smoke in as long as I could, then let it out in the direction of the window. I saw my face in the glass, a scared, pale face, floating in the blackness that was either Kansas or Oklahoma.

I don't know, I said.

Do you think we will?

You mean, like, can I read the future?

She dropped back on her pillow, and lay there staring at the bottom of the upper berth. I knew she wanted me to talk about kids and family and a bunch of other shit I wasn't ready for. Suddenly I was sorry I'd asked her to come.

* * *

I've got a corner room on the third floor, which is the top one. Sea View Apartments, it's called, but you can only see a sliver of the ocean, and only from the window at the other end of the hallway. Every night I listen to Louis, the guy next door, opening and closing his dresser drawers, laying out his clothes for the next morning. I've seen him in a cage at the video arcade on the boardwalk, making change, coming out to fix the machines when they break. We nod to each other, but that's about it. He sees me coming in with girls, and he doesn't ask. He's not around much except late at night. Washing up, running the tap, brushing his teeth: I can hear all that. When he flosses I lie in bed listening to the little clicks the floss makes as he pulls it from between his teeth, and wait for him to run the tap again, and spit twice, and then get into bed.

At least Louis doesn't snore. He must be the only old guy who doesn't. Once he's in bed it's quiet, and I can listen to the sounds coming in through the window, the Atlantic a couple of blocks away smashing against the rocks and the oily pilings of the pier, crickets down in the grass of the vacant lot outside my window. The night train passes a half-mile away, a long disappearing sound headed down the coast to Florida. Every night at eleven, sometimes 11:05, 11:17, once as late as 11:58. I can't sleep until it goes by. Tonight I can't sleep, period. I just keep remembering things, things that happened over thirty years ago. I look at the ceiling in the dark, at the constellations of stick-on Day-Glo stars I put up there. They're pretty much what you'd see if you were looking up at the sky down south during the summer. Hercules, Lyra, Scorpio, the Corona Borealis. They hold a greenish light for a couple of hours after I turn off the switch, and then they fade.

• • •

In Ardmore we set up in the dirt and dry grass behind a shopping center. Hours before, there had been nothing but gnat-ridden air, a litter of fast-food trash, a few scorched places where some bored kids had probably tried to set fires. Now there were the basketball toss and penny pitch, and a shooting gallery full of metal ducks tracking around, ready to topple with any well-aimed blast from the rows of air guns. There were booths of plush bears in bow ties and purple pigs and striped snakes and pinwheels that clacked and glittered. You could whack the Love Meter with a rubber mallet to send the ball straight up its column from Cold Mashed Potato to Red Hot Lover. Beyond the tents the rides looped and plunged, defying the sedate motions of ordinary machines.

My tent was the largest. Out front on a bally stage we had a little black kid in a top hat who made moves like a robot and never cracked a smile. Inside we had a bearded lady, a midget in a tux who played the piano for Dani, whose feather boa turned into a real boa constrictor, and a guy in a diaper who lay on a bed of nails. In the science tent across the way were jars of fetuses: two-headed frogs and goats, animals with six legs that should've had four. Once there had been a guy who bit the heads off live chickens, but that was before my time. I wished I could have seen that. In one of the sideshows, which I turned people toward after my act—Only a dollar more, folks, you don't want to miss this amazing transformation—we had Gorilla Girl, who wore a skimpy fur outfit and stood in a cage and turned into a gorilla through a trick with mirrors. When the gorilla pretended to break out of the cage people would turn and run, sometimes smacking into the big aluminum tent poles. Gorilla Girl had the touch.

Jack and Holly didn't roll in until that evening. I ducked out the back of the tent for a hit off my pipe and saw Holly sitting on the steps of the trailer, fast-smoking a cigarette—drag, exhale, drag, exhale, like she needed to get to the end of it before somebody stopped her—holding a quart bottle of something between her thighs. She had on tight lemon-colored jeans with little silver studs running up the sides, and a ruffled yellow top that left the cream of her shoulders and tops of her breasts exposed. She looked like a banana waiting to be completely peeled. When she looked my way I cupped my hand around the pipe and lowered it. She started toward me, and I ground my thumb into the bowl to kill the fire and slipped it in my pocket.

Want some? she said, dangling the bottle by its neck.

I'd better not. I have one more show to do, I said. The truth was I didn't drink, except for an occasional beer. I couldn't get past the gag reflex that hit me when I even so much as smelled real liquor. The first and only time I'd tried drinking it, in junior high, I got violently sick on my dad's Canadian Club, and then he punched me in the ribs for getting into it.

Only way to get through this shit, Holly said.

Yeah, this is some shit, I said, trying to sound casual. It felt good to say *shit* and not get a dirty look. I felt stupid not accepting a drink, and wondered if Holly thought I wasn't old enough.

How's your act tonight? she asked. She was supposed to be in it, but earlier Jack had conveyed the news that Holly was having her time of the month, as he put it. I wondered if Jack remembered that she'd used her period as an excuse less than two weeks ago.

The act, I said. Great. I wanted to say something tough and worldly, but nothing occurred to me. I looked down at her breasts and then at her wicked little mouth, imagining her doing to me what Alice had only agreed to do twice, and I tried to swell my whole body toward her without actually taking a step in her direction.

You're cute, she said, and reached up and patted my cheek. She looked off, toward the narrow strip of the midway you could see between my tent and the next one. I could hear the *pock-pock* of the airguns, and the rock music from the Scrambler, and yells coming from the Zipper, where people were sent up in cages on long metal arms and flipped upside down while their change and keys fell into the grass. I could hear Holly breathing, a low panting like she'd just been running, and I had the urge to put my ear against her left breast to see how fast her heart was beating; mine was going a million miles an hour.

Have a drink with me, she said, offering the bottle again.

I would have, but I didn't want to gag in front of her. I decided I'd better practice first.

No? she said softly. Little boy doesn't want a grownup drink? she said, in a baby voice. Too bad he doesn't want to play.

Next time, I said. I have to get back.

Promise? she said, still in baby talk.

I wanted to hear her say *Do it to me* in that voice. Promise, I said, backing away from her.

Okay. Bye-bye, she said. She turned and wandered back across the clumps of grass, her heels sinking in with each step. A couple of kids on the Zipper started screaming their heads off.

· · ·

The next place we set up was hardly a town at all. Most of the store windows were boarded up or covered over with newspapers. There was an old movie theater marquee that advertised UMMAGE SALE S ATURDAY. The rides ran without anyone on them. For my noon performance, four people showed—a tired-looking farmer and his wife and their two dusty kids. It was hundred-degree mid-July heat outside, and hotter in the tent. I knew they must have scraped up money for the tickets, and even though Jack wanted to cancel the show and Holly and even Alice said forget it, I insisted.

I had on my ruffled red tuxedo shirt and black velvet bow tie, the microphone around my neck on a bent wire hanger, and I began my spiel, Welcome to the Palace of Illusions, we will amaze you and confuse you, and I acted like the tent was packed with people.

Ladies and gentlemen, I said to the little quartet below me. Today, on this very stage, you will see things you can not, will not, and possibly should not, believe. But you will see that there are more things on heaven and earth than have yet been thought of in your philosophy. I always liked saying that part. I made up my own spiels, from out of my head and bits and pieces of things I'd heard or read.

The farmer hawked tobacco onto the ground, making a loud

sound in his throat first, working it up. His wife leaned back in her chair, hands folded on her fat stomach. Their kids kicked their legs and looked around—at the ceiling of the tent, at Alice holding the dove in two hands.

I threw a white cloth over the dove, turned Alice three times around, and whipped off the cloth to reveal a long-eared white rabbit. I took a bunch of tiny red handkerchiefs, stuffed them into a hole between my thumb and forefinger, and transformed them into one long, sinuous scarf, a hieroglyph of fantastic promise I waved in the stale air. The farmer spat again. The wife closed her eyes. The kids sat there chewing their candy apples. The little boy kicked the girl, not looking at her, and she turned and pinched him. I just kept going. I was sure I'd get them with the guillotine trick.

Holly crouched down behind the guillotine and put her arms through the holes in the stocks—her arms and hands that were supposed to be Alice's. Alice stuck her head through and I stood in front of the guillotine and lowered the fake blade. A little distraction with the cape, and I picked up a box that supposedly had Alice's head in it. Meanwhile, Alice was climbing down underneath the stage on a ladder and crossing to climb back up on the opposite side. I carried the box to a platform with a false bottom and set it down, then Alice stuck her head in from the bottom.

In the stocks, Holly waved her hands around. The hands were supposed to look alike because the women in the audience would usually notice them from when I first brought Alice onstage, notice the shape of her fingers and the color of her nail polish. Alice had been hired partly because she had small freckled hands like Holly's. When Holly didn't feel like doing the act, Jack would have to find a local girl.

I tapped the box with my baton, and the sides fell away, and Alice's head talked.

I feel kind of dizzy, she said.

That's usually when girls screamed and fainted. I guess I wanted to give that family the same feeling, to give those kids something to take home with them and remember when they were older. Something they could believe in, even if only for a fraction of a second, an instant of amazement they could keep, no matter what.

From behind the curtain Dani cranked up the music that signaled the finale, and I strode to the front of the stage and bowed. Sweat dripped off my hair, and my shirt was soaked. I looked down at the four of them. They stood up, but they didn't clap. They just stood there like a little group of cows, the kids working their candy apples in their jaws.

As they shuffled out of the tent Alice gave me a sympathetic look, but Holly came over and punched me in the arm. For a small woman, she hit pretty hard.

What a waste, Holly said.

Leave him alone, Alice said, and moved toward us.

Holly waved her away. Her fingernails were bright red, like Alice's, and they each wore identical fake diamonds on their left hands.

How old are you? Holly asked me. I'm almost thirty, she said. I'm getting too old for this.

Behind her Alice looked at me, and shook her head. I rubbed my arm where Holly had hit me. Alice walked down the stairs off the stage, and out the far end of the tent. I started to follow her, then stopped.

You're not old, I told Holly, though I kind of thought she was. I looked hard at her face, something I'd never really done, at the little lines at the corners of her eyes, and then I thought of how old she'd be when I was nearly thirty, and how those lines would look. But somehow that made her seem even more glamorous, like aging was just stage makeup. I didn't want to get off the stage; I liked being up there, a part of the show.

Maybe if Alice had done something dramatic, screamed at me or punched Holly instead of walking out of the tent, everything would have turned out differently. But what happened was this: I let Holly drag me behind a canvas wall. She stood on a stool and put her little lipsticked mouth all over my mouth and eyelids and neck. I let her lift up my shirt to lick my nipples, and when she took off my cummerbund and pulled my cock from my pants, I was glad her hands didn't feel anything like Alice's.

. . .

Holly could squeeze through the smallest window of opportunity. Every time Jack turned his back for five minutes she'd be sneaking out to meet me. She took to traveling on the train, giving us the opportunity to do it late at night, between cars, the metal plates shifting and grinding beneath my feet while I pushed her against the doors to the caboose.

During stopovers we'd take off after my ten p.m. show, into the fields just beyond the noise and lights of the carnival. The high school couples would be spinning on the Ferris wheel, the guys swinging their feet to make the cars rock wildly so their girlfriends would get scared and cling to them. I'd lie back with my hands behind my head and look up at the stars while Holly jounced up and down on top of me. The idea of art school took on a hazy unreality. I thought instead of wintering in Florida, then heading back to Canada and down through the states in an endless loop, beguiling the crowds, doing the guillotine trick with Holly and some other, anonymous girl.

Holly's favorite place to make love was underneath the Matterhorn ride. You could sneak through a small door in the side and go in among the scaffolding and levers and gears. Above us the music pumped and the kids screamed, whirling past a cheesy painting of the Swiss Alps, while the ride jockey yelled, Do you wanna go faster? The question would be followed by a long, collective squeal of *Yeahhhhh*, and then the screams and shrieks would get even louder. Holly would scream too, *Faster, I wanna go faster*, and I'd put my hand over her mouth to quiet her.

But Holly didn't want to be quiet. Once she screamed when the ride ended, screamed right into the silence between the music stopping and the people climbing out of the cars and clomping down the wooden ramp. I imagined everybody above us knowing exactly what it was—the sound of self-destruction, pure and simple. It was the sound of a train speeding toward a bridge over a deep canyon, a bridge that's been blown up. I heard it, and I knew it, and I fell for her anyway. And after that, when I let her write her name in hickeys on my back, her little mouth sucking until she made the lines of the *H*, the circle of the *O*, the lines and curves of our deceit stretching from one shoulder blade to the other, I knew things were going to get worse and worse.

. . .

In the carnival I learned how to put on a show, and how to steal from people so they didn't know I was doing it. You can count out a handful of bills and make it look like you're giving correct change, but you're not. I learned that some people will believe anything, if you give them half a chance, that some people don't want to look too hard at what you show them. Jack would put his arm around me in a fatherly way as we waited for hot peanuts from the concession stand. He gave me love-making tips, presumably meant for me and Alice, consisting of confusing poker metaphors: don't bet the pot, keep your deuces wild, watch out for the one-eyed queen. Alice helped with the act, and read her medical books, and pretty much ignored the fact that I was coming into our compartment late at night, stuporous from sex and vodka. I had discovered the ancient trick of mixing in a little juice—tomato, grapefruit, cranberry—and had initiated myself, with Holly's help, into the pleasures and requirements of excessive drinking.

That summer when I was twenty-one I shot pictures of Alice reading, painting her nails, leaning over the steel sink in our compartment to shampoo her hair. I thought I could catch her out, somehow—that other Alice who might be inside, waiting to burst forth in sequins and peacock feathers from the quiet, even-tempered Alice. I shot the man stretched on his bed of nails with an overweight woman from the audience straddling his chest, and the cashier who'd been discharged from the Navy with a Section Eight, meaning he was crazy, sitting in his ticket booth with his tattoo-covered arms folded on the counter. I took pictures of Jack, holding the black poodle he walked around with, or eating a bag of french fries drenched in brown gravy. I shot Holly in nothing but her spiked heels, Holly bending forward cradling her nipples in her palms. I knelt over her on a bed in a cheap motel room one afternoon and took photographs while I entered her, pictures of how she looked when we were making love, so that later, when it wasn't real anymore, I would still have her beneath me, her freckles showing through her makeup, the white underneath her arms, the small oval stain someone else had left on the pillow next to her.

All that stuff burned in a fire a couple of years ago. I don't remember how it started, but I was still drinking then.

• • •

In early August, we arrived in Tallahassee. The first night, Holly took off with Jack somewhere, so I found myself at loose ends. I went on the train and checked out the poker game, but there were too many people playing already. I went down the hall to our compartment and knocked before I opened the door.

What do you want, Martin? Alice said, but not like she really wanted to know. She was lying in her berth, reading *Grant's Dissector*. In it, I knew, there were pictures of people being cut open.

Talk to me, I said.

What's the point? Alice said. She didn't lower the book. She talked into its pages, like she was reading aloud from it. You're just going to keep on drinking and being an asshole, she said. Her voice was steady, but I knew she was mad.

You think you're such a big deal, she said. Just because you get on a stage and do some stupid tricks. It doesn't mean anything. It's not real life.

It's better than real life, I said.

How would you know?

I just know.

I want to get married, Alice said. I want to have kids one day.

Me, too, I said. But I was thinking, not yet. I was thinking I had plenty of time. I was thinking that I was in love with Holly, and it felt better than anything I'd had with Alice.

I want to get married, Alice said again.

To me?

No. She finally put the book down, and looked at me. I want to go home, she said. I can't take this shit anymore.

So the next day I walked her over to the Greyhound station. I bought her a Tab and a Snickers bar from the machines. In the warped mirror of the candy machine I looked weird, my face elongated, my long hair too bushy and thick. Alice sat on a molded orange plastic seat with her suitcase beside her and an enormous panda bear on her lap, a present for her little sister.

A farewell photo, I said, raising my camera.

Martin, she said, and I took the shot, Alice's head down, the panda bear's shining glass eyes, the blur of her raised palm saying, *Don't*.

That night I went alone into town, to a place called the Do Drop Inn, and drank until the pour spout of the Smirnoff bottle the bartender had set on the counter doubled itself. I headed back to the train, to the compartment without Alice in it, and took a picture of her empty berth, the depression in the pillow made by her head. I smoked some pot and shot the smoke spiraling up, and drank some more vodka from a bottle I had nearly finished, and kicked the bottle across the compartment and watched it ricochet back. I got out the .38 Jack had given me after the incident with the Hell's Angels, and lay on Alice's berth holding it, wondering if it was loaded. At our last stopover the Angels had been drinking beer out of their helmets and generally being rowdy, and one had climbed onstage to try and kiss the local girl who was putting her arms through the stocks. The whole place had closed down instantly, the carnies coming up the midway with pipes and chains. Jack escorted the Angels to the gates with a pump shotgun. Afterwards he said I should have protection. At first I thought he was talking about condoms, and I was sure he knew about me and Holly. Jack was a big man, and I'd always been a little scared of him. Seeing him wave that shotgun at the Hell's Angels made me sweat. He handed me the .38 and patted my shoulder. Don't go shooting this off without provocation, he said. Keep it in your pants, he said, and I mumbled a thank you and walked off.

I put the gun on Alice's pillow and took its picture, and then I felt like finding Holly and something more to drink.

She was sitting out front of their trailer in a folding chair. I saw the bright spark of her cigarette zigging back and forth, fast, as usual, and smelled the mixture that was her, smoke and Jack Daniels and face cream.

What the fuck, she said, I've been looking for you all night. Alice left.

Oh baby, I'm sorry. Come inside, Holly said, getting up. She moved toward me and I stepped back.

Listen, she said. When the summer's over, we'll take off. I know where Jack keeps his cash. We can just go—wherever we go. She waved her cigarette, like it was going to illuminate a path for us.

I'm planning on art school.

I like art. I'll go, too. She dropped her cigarette in the dirt and came over, and put her face against my shirt. I need you, she said.

Jack, I said.

Still counting the day's receipts, she said. She took a handful of my shirt and gently pulled me toward the trailer. I followed her inside, past the kitchenette. She found the gun in my back pocket, took it out, and set it on the nightstand. Then she pulled me down onto the bed.

She started kissing my neck, moving underneath me. I remembered the way she had sounded that night weeks ago, out back of my tent, that sweet voice, and I let her unbelt my pants and helped her pull off my boots. Soon we were naked and making love.

That was when Jack showed up, carrying his little poodle under one arm, and said, It figures.

After that, things happened kind of fast. I rolled off Holly. She was screaming Shit, shit, shit, shit. I looked at Jack and there was something sticking out of his pocket. Maybe I saw it was the black handle of a screwdriver and not a gun, and maybe

I didn't know for sure. I don't know what I was thinking. That if it weren't for Jack, Holly and I could be together. That I wanted Jack to disappear. That he had caught me and Holly and I was in for it. Maybe that's what I thought later, and not in those few seconds. I grabbed the gun, turned wildly, and fired. The gun sounded louder than a gun should, in the close air of the trailer. It kicked and my hand jerked up. Jack staggered backwards, toward the built-in bench on the far wall. He dropped the dog.

·   ·   ·

Tonight, after I got the news about Holly, I took a walk on the boardwalk. There are rides at the end, past the noisy video arcade where Louis works, past the booths with the same prizes they've always had, but I never go as far as the rides. I go as far as Guess Your Weight and Age, a booth like the one I worked in for twenty years, after I got out of prison and hooked up with a different carnival. That's where I found this girl, a little sixteen-year-old who obviously thought she looked much older in her short skirt and heels. She won a pink bear from the kid at the booth—he guessed nineteen—but I could tell she was in high school, or should have been. I asked her to pose for me. I told her she had model potential. She looked me over and said okay, and I bought her a slice of pizza on the way up.

I don't touch the girls. I just take pictures and give them some money and ask them to sign a release saying they're over eighteen, whether they are or not, and I turn around and sell their nakedness for a little more money to a guy who has an Internet site.

I also have a running ad in the paper for weddings. Now and then I'll get a call to show up at a church or someone's backyard, and I'll spend the day taking the usual poses, like the bride and groom about to cut the cake, her hand over his on the knife so the rings show. If they want film, I do that, and then I sell them the negatives. Most people don't care anymore about film, though, so most of the time I put everything on a thumb drive or CD, and hand it over. Then I'm done, no expensive packages to convince them to buy. My services are cheap, and they're still getting a professional, which they like.

When I take pictures of the girls I think of the men who will look at them and not know how their voices sounded, how they brushed the hair out of their eyes, how they were timid or afraid or sometimes proud, men who don't care who they're looking at. Sandy, Lily, Jane, Maria. I can put a name to every face, every pair of breasts. I remember which one was beaten by her father and which one wanted to work in radio and which one left crying in the middle of the shoot. They're all pretty, and they all really could be models. I try to give them that hope, to show them that someone saw something special in them. In a way it's just like shooting weddings. The camera captures them at their best. Those newlyweds, they'll be fighting soon. Disappointment is what they have to look forward to.

• • •

I gave the girl a few more instructions: lean back on your elbows, open your mouth. Just writhe around a little, do whatever. She had Holly's body, the narrow waist, breasts that looked too heavy for her. She had that sweet voice, that sounded more innocent than it was.

Holly's liver gave out, Don John had said on the phone. He coughed again. He's got cancer, but he's still smoking. Last I heard, he said, she was hooking in Vegas. You can bet it wasn't any place like the Mirage or New York, New York, Don John said. Don John always kept track of Holly. The last time he told me about her he said she had arthritis. Her hands looked like Lobster Girl's, he'd said. Once I asked him if she ever asked about me, and he let a couple of heartbeats go by before he said, Yeah, sure, all the time.

The manager of some hotel found her, Don John said. Anyway, he said. I thought you'd want to know.

This girl I photographed tonight had on too much makeup. She opened her legs like she had something inside her, something besides a great emptiness needing to be filled.

I could do something else for you, she said. For a little more money.

I don't want that, I told her.

I don't mind, she said. Honestly.

I knew how good she'd feel, and I wanted to go over to the bed, to put my hands on her and hear her moan. I thought of how Louis, if he were in his room, would hear her. But he wasn't there. No one was there but me and this girl, and I could have done what I wanted with her. I could have released this feeling into her, instead of lying here with it now.

I've done it before, she said. I'm not as young as you think.

I know how old you are, I said. Just stay still.

This girl, I didn't ask her name. I was tired, and I didn't need to know her story. I took one more picture. I held her in the frame of my camera, just for an instant, an instant in which I might have loved her, and then I let her go.

IN THE TIME OF THE BYZANTINE EMPIRE

Her ex-husband had been in a terrible accident. Biking alone in the Hudson Valley, he had lost control on a downhill and crashed into a tree, breaking several ribs and his scapula. He'd been wearing a helmet but had sustained a brain injury. Now their son had flown up from D.C. to New York to be with him; his present wife was constantly by his side, through the ICU and emergency surgery, through the hospital stay and the move to a rehab facility where he was learning, slowly, to identify photographs of animals and the names of the people who surrounded him. There were a lot of people; he was a popular language professor, regarded as a leading translator of contemporary Slavic verse. One of his books was widely used as a textbook. He had a stream of visitors when he was able to have them, and many offers of support from students, colleagues, and friends.

The ex-wife knew this from the blog a teaching assistant had set up on a Web site called Caring Heart. She was in Italy, on sabbatical, working on an architectural book about

Ravenna. She had been spending her time thinking about sepulchers made of porphyry and the fates of Byzantine monarchs, watching the light reflect off the gold haloes of martyred saints walking in a bright mosaic procession toward Jesus and Mary and the angels. Her thoughts had been centered on churches and basilicas, and on a restaurant where she often ate and where she drank, most evenings, a Campari spritz followed by a carafe of red wine. She would go home to the apartment she rented, not far from where Byron had once lived with Teresa Guicciolo. There she would have more wine, enough to allow her to pass into a restless sleep before waking in the middle of the night, sweating from a hot flash. She would read for an hour or so, and then, if she couldn't get back to sleep, would tap out a Xanax, swallow half with a glass of *acqua minerale*, and thereby lose another morning of work.

Now she spent those late moments of the night on Caring Heart, reading about her former husband. The entries were written by his assistant and a close colleague, and sometimes by his wife. He was agitated, and had pulled out all the tubing and tried to rise from bed; he was calm and serene and loving, or angry and sarcastic. He called his son by his dead brother's name, and pulled the covers over his head and refused to eat, or struggled forward with a walker, making it halfway down the hall. There were loving messages from everyone he knew; the ex-wife, herself, had written a couple of them: *Wishing you a fast recovery. Thinking of you all during this difficult time.*

What she felt, but did not write, was that she was jealous. It was a dark, self-pitying jealousy, and it moved like a black wave over all the images that passed through her mind, leaving behind its bitter salt.

Their son had once been angry with his father, in his late adolescence, but that had long passed, and for the past several years they had enjoyed a close relationship. Her own relationship with her son had gone from an easy intimacy (he had been hers alone as a baby and toddler, while her husband was busy with teaching) to a distant politeness that frustrated her, and that she did not understand. Her son treated her as a casual acquaintance, one he did not particularly want to know further; he rarely called or wrote. While she, as always with her emotions, was overwhelmed by their ferocity and did her best to tamp them down to an acceptable level. Otherwise, she noticed, people tended to edge away from her, as though a glass had just shattered at their feet. Now her son was closer to his father than ever. The entries on the Web site often mentioned the word *family*, the family being, of course, her ex-husband, their son, and the wife of the past ten years. The three of them were like a beautiful painting or fresco, perfectly proportioned, luminous with religious meaning. Mary flanked by two hovering angels, or holding her veil playfully above an infant Jesus while Joseph stood meditatively in the background. The hand of God, the suffering Christ, and the white dove. Whereas she, the ex, was one. An aberration. She was a drunken apostate.

Her former husband was a good man, and she had screwed up the marriage. The last year they were together, she had begun an affair with one of his graduate students. She had lied about where she went, invented a friend named Veronica who often needed her, had come home from fucking her lover all afternoon straight into the shower and then to the living room to greet her husband. She could not remember, now, why she had done these things. There had been a vague but persistent dissatisfaction, a longing for—but she never knew what. She had finally told him about the affair; her lover had left her, she was (she thought) miserably in love, she might (she also thought) get back together with her lover, without the obstacle of the marriage. Their son was twelve at the time. She had screwed up her relationship with him, too, and for what? Afterwards there had been a handful of men, including one who was married, who had at one time promised to leave his wife, who did not leave, and she found herself alone.

· · ·

In Ravenna, there were bicycles everywhere, and no one wore a helmet. Every day, she was reminded of her ex-husband. It was unclear how many of his abilities he might regain after the insult to his brain. Everyone was trying to be upbeat and hopeful. The doctors had said that full recovery was unlikely. She remembered what a kind, fair man he had been; even after he knew about the infidelity, and the marriage was over, he had shared care of their son and been generous in terms of finances. It hurt her to think that now he would be reduced; he might not be able to return to teaching, or even care for himself.

Today, she learned from his wife's entry on Caring Heart, he was going to be forced to leave the rehab facility. Their insurance would not pay for him to stay longer. He would need round-the-clock care for an indefinite amount of time. People were volunteering to run errands, offering money and places to stay. The wife wrote that sometimes it was all too much for her. *I want him back the way he was*, she wrote. The ex-wife felt incredibly mean of spirit, but there it was, that thick, viscous surge of feeling: she still envied the wife. The wife who today was packing up his things, helping him out the glass doors, taking him home. They would have a quiet dinner with her son, who was staying with them as long as he was needed. He would sit with his iPad in the living room, near his father on the couch. His father would have his stocking feet on the coffee table; maybe he would be trying to decipher a book, or simply be leaning back against the cushions, tired and drawn-looking; every now and then a small ripple of confusion would pass over his face, and then subside. She did not want to be on the outside, feeling like a voyeur to his suffering. She wanted to be, again, a part of what they had had together, what she had foolishly thrown away.

She read the wife's journal entry at five a.m. and could not get back to sleep, even with an entire Xanax. She lay in the dark remembering the early years of her marriage. She had slept beside her husband easily, insensibly, night after night, never waking. In the mornings she would curl against his back, and he would reach behind and pull her arm around him. He would come home from his classes and drop a stack of books and papers on the dining room table, where he liked to work. They would cook dinner together, drinking wine he would have opened while telling her about the vintage or the origins of the wine, then pouring her a bit to taste before he filled their glasses. Soon their son would be born, and she would cradle him in the crook of her arm as she stirred soup or risotto, or put him in his playpen, where he would lie looking up at a mobile of plush farm animals in his solemn way. Their young family—husband, wife, new son—had seemed inviolable, like a photograph or painting; in her memory it was still there, perfectly framed, glassed-in and inaccessible.

Around seven a.m. she rose, exhausted, and walked down the street for a cappuccino and croissant at her usual café. She went to another café on the Via di Roma for a second cappuccino and tried to read a monograph on medieval iconography, but mostly she sat, looking out the window, thinking about her former life. It had been a good life. She had destroyed it, and out of that her husband had built a new one. She had built nothing. After Ravenna she would go back to Boston to the small studio apartment she owned, where she lived with an ailing cat and a wall of shelves filled with books, where a folding futon doubled as bed and couch. She put her elbows on the table and leaned over her cappuccino, letting her hair fall over her face so the other patrons would not see that she was crying.

A little later she crossed over to Sant'Apollinare Nuovo. She always felt stirred by the glitter of the mosaics, the marble columns, the coffered ceiling and soffits of the arches. The basilica had been built at the beginning of the sixth century by an Ostrogoth conqueror, Theodoric, as an Arian chapel for his palace. Some of the mosaics at one end of the nave had once depicted the king and his court. Fifty years later, when Theodoric was dead and Ravenna was under Byzantine rule, the church had been reconsecrated as a Catholic one, and the figures had been covered over with images of curtains. What had been Theodoric on his throne was now a gold design. There was only one visible indication of the change that had occurred: a hand from one of the original figures had been left. Slim and white, the hand came out of the darkness between two curtains and rested against a column, barely noticeable from below unless you knew it was there.

She gazed up at it until her neck hurt. She began to imagine a very still, silent, somehow living figure hidden behind the bright tiles, breathing quietly—maybe a lady-in-waiting in a richly colored brocade gown. The figure would feel the light coming through the arched windows on the east side of the nave, hot on her open palm and the cuff of her sleeve. The rest of her would be achingly cold. She would have stood there year after year, enduring her own erasure. One day she might step forward and show herself. She might drift down through the hushed air, past the startled tourists, and step lightly onto the marble floor. Then she would walk out into the open courtyard, where a palace had once been, and feel the sun on her face again.

BLOWN

Ｙou're having breakfast with a boy you slept with last night but don't know very well. In fact, you don't know him at all; you met in a bar near campus, the kind you usually don't go into—peanut shells littering the floor, pool tables between you and the ladies' room, not a potted fern or plate glass window anywhere—and you let him talk you into going back to his place. Not for a nightcap. You sense the word *nightcap* would be as unlikely to cross his lips as *motif*, or *semiotics,* or *Deux ex machina*. No, what he said was, "You wanna go hang at my spot?" You had drunk enough margaritas with Amaretto floaters to nod, dumbly. You would have dogsledded with him across a cracking ice floe, followed him into an ebola epidemic, tribal warfare; what you did was stumble to a stucco house two blocks away, through a dirt yard and past an enormous American flag serving as a curtain for the picture window, into your latest ill-advised erotic encounter.

This morning you gave him a blow job, then felt nauseous, ran to the bathroom with a blanket wrapped around you in case any of his roommates were home, and threw up. It was probably due to all the tequila last night, but still. It seemed rude, to swallow someone's come and then race from the room, gagging, to kneel in front of the toilet.

At breakfast there are long silences. You keep your sunglasses on. He's so beautiful you want to weep—he's so beautiful you know you can't have him. You want to own him, like a pet, to drag him back to your room with you and not let him leave the dorm except in your company.

He lives in a room with peeling wallpaper the color and texture of a Triscuit. You remember a mattress on the floor, a pile of dirty laundry by the mattress, a couple of ants crawling over the current issue of *Car and Driver*. There wasn't a single book in the room, unless you counted an ancient Yellow Pages sprawled in the corner, bloated from water, as though it had been rescued from the toilet down the hall. In the bathroom was a pile of *Hustlers* with his name on the subscription labels. You can't believe that you, an English Literature major at an extremely well-regarded private college, licked the balls of someone who doesn't read. You look at him across the table, at his dark hair falling in his eyes, and wonder if he likes you.

Last night the two of you talked nonstop. You try to remember what you talked about, but all you can call up is some comment he made about liking your blue cowboy boots, and a comparison of your drug histories. He smoked pot twice and once ate a Vicodin by accident. You spent your senior year of high school stoned, and did so much Ecstasy you had to be hospitalized over Spring Break. Your head starts hurting so you give up trying to remember anything. Don't think. Focus on the present. Why doesn't he say anything? Why does he just sit there, looking like a god, drinking tea from a tall glass embellished with—it can't be, but you see now there are naked women on the glass. You look around the restaurant, but there's nothing to hint at pornographic glassware. There are two large, badly executed oil paintings: one of wild horses, and another of wild geese. The horses are doomed to extinction, the geese have nowhere to fly but into the wall. Ordinary glass salt and pepper shakers adorn the tables. The women on his drinking glass aren't drawn on, but—how would you say it?— blown. Their breasts and bellies protrude. He lifts them to his lips. You can feel yourself getting wet, and you shift in your seat.

You can't stand the silence any longer so you say, "Are you always so quiet when you come?" He barely made a sound this morning as you knelt before him, the mattress buttons digging into your knees. You're a very verbal person, usually, and you get paranoid when people don't talk. Maybe he was gritting his teeth this morning, wishing he'd never invited you in. Maybe he's sitting there now thinking the same thing you're thinking: my God, what have I done? He shifts in his seat now, too, and lowers his eyes like he's embarrassed. The waitress is suddenly there with your breakfast, and you can see by the look on her face she heard your question, or at least the phrase *when you come*, and you lower your own eyes to the plate she sets in front of you.

You try again to remember something, anything, from last night's conversation. Surely there must be some common ground. There was a discussion about prisoners asking for kosher meals—who had brought that one up? "What do they think it is, summer camp?" he had said. "It's prison! Feed 'em slop." This comment had made you extremely anxious, so you drank another shot of tequila. By this time you were at his kitchen table, trying to put together a two-piece child's wooden puzzle. The pieces were supposed to form a pyramid. You spent half an hour or so fruitlessly turning them at various angles to each other, unable to figure it out, until he finally showed you. Of course it was simple; a matter of changing your perception slightly, and the trick became obvious. This is how your sexual life often feels—things almost fit, but you don't seem to have the knack of looking at them in the right way. You have long periods of no boyfriend, then there are too many and you can't choose. You love boys who leave you. The ones who love you don't satisfy you sexually. You go home with illiterate people who probably, if they knew the first thing about you, would want you locked up and fed slop.

You eat your eggs and English muffin, and they taste like glue. You can't remember who made the first move last night, when the sexual tension slid into actual fucking. Don't call it lovemaking. He didn't even ask if you came; you didn't. He said you were pretty before he fell asleep, one arm across your breasts like an iron bar. You try to think of analogies from literature, of stories in which an unlikely prospect ends up being the love of a girl's life, and realize that despite your expensive first-class education, your heart is busy living in a crackerbox apartment, reading cheesy romance novels on the burn-holed couch, getting fat on Mr. Pretzels and Little Debbie cupcakes.

It's obvious that this boy is a simpleton, a dullard, a *bête noir*; in short, not to put too fine a point on it, a dumbass. You can see this clearly in the buzzy fluorescent glare of the restaurant, watching the way he fondles the women on his glass with his ignorant, thickly padded fingers. You realize you are going to have to tell him—right now, or, okay, maybe in a text tomorrow—that you can't ever see him again. You lift your fork and stare at his mouth. He smiles; he has big beautiful teeth, perfectly even and white, like tablets you could write your autobiography on, if you could write small enough, and just like that, the next seven months of your life go down the drain.

THE HAG'S JOURNEY

Once there was a hag who was really a princess, who lived in a storage unit that was really a castle. In summer the unit was very hot, so she kept the corrugated metal door open to catch the breeze and set a fan just outside on the asphalt of her yard. The asphalt was really a beach, the grains of sand fine and white, silken as the hair of a baby, for in fact, the sand really was a baby. Most of the time, it lay very still; it was a good baby, not fussy at all, for inside it was a dewy flower, and flowers are happy unless they are being cut away from the earth and tied with twine or rubber bands to other flowers, then imprisoned in vases, soon to droop and brown and be thrown into a large, foul-smelling plastic bin. There was just such a bin outside the hag's door. Inside, though it was full of things like shriveled flowers and old tax returns, the bin was empty.

The hag who was really a princess was unhappy in her castle, because what good is a princess with a castle unless there is a prince somewhere, dropping a sweaty T-shirt on the floor or putting together a lounge chair ordered off the Internet or snoring like a house on fire? For a prince's snores are really, in the end, the smoke of burning things, photo albums and funny gifts and Post-Its on the refrigerator. But there had been no prince for ten thousand years. The hag had looked for one in vain, among the frogs and snails that lived nearby, and especially she had looked for one each time it rained and the little square of grass she had laid as a welcome mat at the entrance to the castle grew sodden, and worms slithered up from the loosened soil and lay there panting from the effort, enjoying the soft caresses of the rain. The worms seemed promising. But when the sun came out again, they disappeared, or dried out and died and turned to brittle twigs.

The hag determined to go on a quest, for it appeared that no prince was going to wander past the storage unit and be struck dumb by her beauty, which anyway was difficult to see unless he had been drugged with the right potion by another hag, and in that case he was likely to be taken already, locked up in that other hag's storage unit. So she put on her old coat that smelled of mothballs and moldy bread, a coat that wished it were really a magic cloak; but unfortunately for the coat, it was really only a horse blanket, and though it could wish as much as it wanted, nothing would be granted to it, and the horse was wandering the earth elsewhere.

The hag packed a basket filled with objects that might tempt a prince to come to her, if she encountered one and he happened to be shy. There were several red, wet-mouthed smiles wrapped in tissue paper, a bottle of potion that required no corkscrew, and an extra large five-cheese pepperoni pizza. There was a small blue bird that could startle out at a moment's notice, become a handkerchief, and flutter prettily to the ground. It was the usual stuff, nothing fancy, but she couldn't afford the higher-end basket, which came with seasonal fruit and flattering lighting and chocolates that turned to nipples at the touch of a prince's tongue. Still she set out, hopeful and a little nervous about venturing into the woods alone.

After several months of traveling, sleeping on the ground and sometimes finding shelter with a witch or inside a hollow tree, the hag spotted a prince. He was meditating in a little clearing where a unicorn was peacefully grazing. Though the hag was generally scornful of superstition, of signs and so-called miracles, the unicorn struck her as a good omen. The prince was so handsome, his handsome legs so defined beneath his tights, his equally handsome arms and hands oiled and shining like armor, that the hag was afraid to approach him at first. She watched him meditate for an hour or so, and when he finally opened his eyes she got up the courage to move toward him, quietly flipping open the wooden basket lid on its little hinge so the blue bird could startle out and flutter prettily to the ground. Which it did.

"Allow me," the prince said, bounding to his feet to pick up the handkerchief. He returned it to her with a graceful bow, sweeping his cap off his head and then holding it against his handsome chest. Once he had drunk most of the potion and eaten the still-piping-hot pizza and sampled a few of the red, wet-mouthed smiles, he was hers. He was a very young prince, it hardly needs to be pointed out; he had never seen such wonders as the hag who was really a princess showed him.

The prince and the princess returned to her castle and lived there happily ever after, though ever after was actually a fairly short time, only a year or so. The princess kept a good supply of potion on hand, and there were frequent deliveries of pizza, but the wet-mouthed smiles were growing scarce. The market could not keep them in stock, so she often had to make do with tight smiles, or smiles of feigned interest, and sometimes there were none at all. Once upon a time, the prince had seen the hag for the princess she actually was. Now, he had begun to see that inside the princess a smaller, haglike creature hunkered down, with messy hair that hissed and wailed and sometimes tied itself into knots. No self-respecting princess would allow herself such terrible hair days. And it turned out that the prince, so handsome and loving and kind, housed a weak, pale worm deep in the apple of his soul. It weakly but steadily ate its way out of him, while the hag inside the princess inside the hag began to grow like a glioblastoma.

One sunny morning, the prince ate his breakfast, made now mostly from leftover frowns and sullen glances, then stepped outside, smoked a quick cigarette, and ground it into the sand with his princely boot. He called for the unicorn with a secret signal, and was on its back and gone in an instant. Behind him, the castle filled with smoke. The hag ran to and fro, waving her cloak and crying. The tears hissed as they fell, and left little holes in the dishtowels and sheets. In a fit of rage and grief, the hag strangled the princess inside her until the princess turned purple and her eyes bulged and her shining hair fell out in big clumps and she shit all over herself and lay still forever.

Out of the princess's shit crawled a teeny old woman, slightly dazed. She blinked at the hag and held out to her a jar filled with warm water. At the bottom of the jar lay a handful of golden seeds.

"Wait for these to sprout, and then plant them in your garden, and they will bring you happiness," she said.

"Impossible. Nothing will ever make me happy again," said the hag, more than ever wary of superstitions, of signs and so-called miracles.

But this being a tale, nothing was impossible. "They will make you happy," the teeny old woman insisted.

Which, eventually, after another ten thousand years, they did. The hag's garden flourished with all manner of strange and interesting flowers. The basket that had accompanied her on her last journey was now set into the earth, beside a stone fountain whose water tinkled like fairy pee, and was a perfect spot to grow basil.

And what of the blue bird, that could startle out and float down so prettily, inspiring the gallantry and solicitousness of strangers? It flew off to live on a nearby light pole that was actually a tall, ancient tree. It sang sometimes in an unpleasant voice, sounding like a hinge that needed oiling. In cold weather, it tucked its small blue head under one wing. It may have wept, but even the mites who inhabited it could not tell if that was so. Every year, during summer thunderstorms, worms wriggled to the surface of the earth, and the bird watched them luxuriating in the garden, beneath the soft caresses of the rain, and then it swooped down to impale them.

EVER AFTER

The loft where the dwarfs lived had a view of the city and hardwood floors and skylights, but it was overpriced, and too small now that there were seven of them. It was a fifth-floor walkup, one soaring, track-lighted room. At the far end was the platform where Doc, Sneezy, Sleepy, and Bashful slept side by side on futons. Beneath them, Happy and Dopey shared a double bed. Grumpy, who pretty much stayed to himself, kept his nylon sleeping bag in a corner during the day and unrolled it at night on the floor between the couch and the coffee table. The kitchen was two facing zinc counters, a built-in range and microwave, and a steel refrigerator, all hidden behind a long bamboo partition that Doc had bought and Sneezy had painted a color called Cherry Jubilee. The kitchen and bathroom were the only places any sort of privacy was possible. To make the rent they all pooled their money from their jobs at the restaurant, except for Dopey, who didn't have a job unless you counted selling drugs when he wasn't running them up his arm; and Grumpy, who panhandled every day for spare change and never came up with more than a few wrinkled dollar bills when the first of the month rolled around. Sometimes the rest of them talked about kicking out Dopey and Grumpy, but no one quite had the heart. Besides, the Book said there were seven when she arrived, seven disciples of the goddess who would come with the sacred apple and transform them. How, exactly, they would be transformed was a mystery that would be revealed when she got there. In the meantime, it was their job to wait.

"When she comes, she'll make us big," said Sneezy. He had the comics section of the Sunday paper, and an egg of Silly Putty, and was flattening a doughy oval onto a panel of Calvin and Hobbes.

"Oh, bullshit," said Grumpy. "It's about *inner* transformation, man. That's the whole point. Materialism is a trap. Identifying with your body is a trap. All this shit"—Grumpy swept his arm to indicate not just their loft but the tall downtown buildings beyond the windows, shimmering in the July heat, and maybe more—"is an illusion. Maya. Samsara." He shook out the last Marlboro from a pack, crumpled the pack, and tried a hook shot into a wicker wastebasket by the window, but missed. He looked around. "Matches? Lighter? Who's going for more cigs?"

"She will," insisted Sneezy. "She'll make us six feet tall if we want to be."

"She can't change genetics, you dope," Grumpy said.

At the word dope, Dopey's head jerked up for an instant. He was nodding on the couch at the opposite end from Grumpy, a lit cigarette ready to fall from his hand. The couch had a few burn holes already. One of these days, Doc thought, he's going to set the fucking place on fire, and then where will we be? How will she ever find us?

He got up from the floor, where he'd been doing yoga stretches, and slid the cigarette from Dopey's stained fingers. He ground it out in an ashtray on the table, in the blue ceramic water of a moat that circled a ceramic castle. From the castle's tiny windows, a little incense smoke—sandalwood—drifted out.

"She's not an alien from outer space who's going to perform weird experiments," Doc said. He hunted through the newspaper for the Food section.

"Where is she from, then?" Sneezy said. Sneezy was a sixteen-year-old runaway, the youngest of them. From the sweet credulousness of his expression, you'd never know what terrible things he had endured. He'd been beaten, scarred between his shoulder blades with boiling water, forced into sex with his mother by his own father. Sneezy liked to ask the obvious questions for the sake of receiving the familiar, predictable answers.

"She's from the castle," Doc said. "She's the fairest in the land. She will come with the sacred apple and all will be changed." This much the Book said. *Once upon a time,* it said. But when was that, exactly? Doc wondered. They'd been here for over six years already. Or he had, anyway. Ever since he'd found the Book in a Dumpster—the covers ripped away, most of its pages stained and torn—where he'd been looking for food a nearby restaurant always threw out. He'd been on the streets, addicted to cheap wine, not giving a shit about anything or anyone. He'd slept on cardboard in doorways, with a Buck knife under the rolled poncho he used for a pillow, and had stolen children's shoes from outside the Moon Bounce at the park. He had humiliated himself performing drunken jigs in the bank plaza for change tossed into a baseball cap. The Book had changed all that. It had shown him there was a purpose to his life. To gather the others, to come to this place and make it ready. He had quit drinking and found a job, at the very restaurant whose Dumpster he used to scrounge through. He had gathered his brethren, one by one, as they drifted into the city from other places, broke and down on their luck, headed for the streets and shelters. They had become his staff—two dishwashers, a busboy, and a fry cook. The restaurant's name was Oz, and the owner had been willing to hire dwarf after dwarf and present them as ersatz munchkins. There had been a feature article in the *Weekly*, and write-ups in some food magazines, which had drawn a lot of business. The dwarfs were mentioned in the guidebooks, so there were often tourists from Canada and Denmark and Japan who brought their cameras to record the enchanting moment the dwarfs trooped from the kitchen with a candlelit torte to stand around a table and sing "Happy Birthday." They used fake high voices, as though they'd been sucking on helium.

"Why is the apple sacred?" Sneezy said dreamily. He had abandoned the comics and now had a few Magic cards spread out on the floor and was picking them up one by one, studying them.

"Because she will die of the apple and be resurrected," Doc said. He glanced at one of Sneezy's cards: Capashen Unicorn. An armored unicorn raced through a sparkling field, a white-robed rider on its back. Underneath, Doc read: *Capashen riders were stern and humorless even before their ancestral home was reduced to rubble.*

"Why do you collect that crap?" Doc said. "And those comic books you've always got your nose buried in. Read the Book again. Every time I read it, I discover something new. The Book is all you need. You have to focus on the Book."

"Check her out." Sneezy held up another card, of an anorectic-looking woman with green skin in a gold ballerina outfit. One long-nailed thumb and forefinger were raised in the air in some kind of salute. In her other hand she held aloft a green and white flag. A couple of men in armor rode behind her, and behind them rose broccoli-like trees, being erased by mist rising out of the ground. Doc read: *Llanowar Vanguard. Creature—Dryad. Llanowar rallied around Eladamri's banner and united in his name.*

"Will she look like that?" Sneezy asked.

"Give it a rest," Grumpy said, and nudged Dopey with his foot. "Hey, man," he said. "We're out of cigs."

Sneezy will outgrow it, Doc thought. Dryads and unicorns. Made-up creatures and clans and battles. "I don't know what she'll look like, exactly," he sighed. He stood up and began tidying the coffee table. Empty semi-crushed cans of Bud Light that Grumpy and Dopey had drunk the night before. A half-eaten bag of tortilla strips. A plastic tub of salsa had spilled on the naked body of a Penthouse Pet. The magazine lay open to her spread legs, her long, slender fingers teasingly positioned above her pink slit; it glistened, as though it had been basted. What would she look like? Maybe she would look like this, would come and drag her fingers through the graying hair on his chest and position her sweet eager hips above him. Maybe she would whisper to Doc that he was the one she came for, the only one; they could leave all the others behind, now that she was there. They would leave the city and move to an Airstream in the woods, overlooking a little river, where he could catch bass and bluegills. She would stand in front of their stove in cutoffs and a white blouse, sliding a spatula under a fish sputtering in a pan. When the moon rose, the two of them would go down to the river and float together, naked. Their heads would be the same height above the water.

Doc closed the magazine. He gathered up the beer cans, carried them into the kitchen, and threw them on top of the pile of trash overflowing from the can.

• • •

The next afternoon he left a note on the refrigerator, securing it with a magnet Bashful had bought, of the Virgin Mary's stroller with the baby Jesus riding in it. The magnet set included Mary in a nightgown, her hands raised in prayer, with several changes of clothes and accessories including a skateboard, waitress uniform, flowered pants and hippie shirt, a plaid skirt, and roller skates. Right now Mary just had on the nightgown and was riding the skateboard. Another magnet, of a small Magic 8 Ball, had been stuck over her face.

House Meeting 7 PM, Doc had written. *Important!!! Please everyone. I'll buy the beer.* He knew that would ensure that Grumpy and Dopey showed.

Dopey didn't arrive until 7:30, strolling in with a bag of peanut M&M's. But at least they were all there, with a couple of six-packs and cigarettes and Nacho Cheese Doritos in a bowl on the table, the windows open to the hot night air. Doc was drinking his usual, Caffeine Free Diet Coke. Bashful passed around a large order of McDonald's fries and unwrapped a Big Mac. Crap, Doc thought, watching him eat, but it smelled pretty good, and he couldn't resist a couple of the fries.

"Why do we need a house meeting?" Grumpy said. "I got things to do." He hadn't shaved in a while, and his black beard stubble went halfway down his neck. Not so long ago, Doc remembered, Grumpy used to shave every day, no matter what.

"Oh, I love house meetings," Happy said. Happy loved nearly everything. He loved communal living and being a bus-boy at Oz. He loved being one of the Chosen who had been selected to wait. He loved the Book and would defend it when anyone criticized it, which seemed to be more and more often lately. Just a couple of days ago, Sleepy, who was taking a community college class, had come home talking nonsense. "It's like the Bible," he said. "It's, like, a metaphor or something. You know the cross? Jesus on the cross? The professor said the cross is really like a pagan fertility symbol." Sleepy had no idea what a metaphor was, though. When pressed, he couldn't define symbol, either. "You don't know what you're saying," Happy had concluded, and Doc explained to Sleepy that the Book was nothing like the Bible. The Bible was meant for normals, Doc said, but the Book was for dwarfs.

"I called the meeting," Doc said, "because I'm sick of picking up after all of you. Sleepy cleaned the bathroom and left soap streaks all over the mirror. I can barely see myself in it. And you, Grumpy, you and Dopey—all you do is strew beer cans and cigarette butts and fast-food trash from one end of this place to the other. And this morning Bashful put the dishes from the dishwasher back in the cupboards when they hadn't even been washed yet."

"Sorry," Bashful muttered.

"I have to do everything around here," Doc said.

"Don't be such a goddamned martyr," Grumpy said, popping his second bottle of Red Hook.

"You should try pulling your own weight for once," Doc said. "Don't think we're going to carry you forever."

"Oh, but we love you, Grumpy," Happy said. He put his hand on Grumpy's shoulder. "You're the bomb," Happy said, using an expression he'd picked up from Sneezy.

"Get your paw off me," Grumpy said. "Freak."

"Look who's talking." Happy had an edge in his voice now. The one thing Happy didn't love was being a dwarf. At four foot ten, Happy was the closest to normal-sized, and Doc often wondered if Happy stayed, not only because of his dedication to the Book, but because this was the only place he got to be bigger than everyone else.

"I don't need you freaks," Grumpy said, giving Happy a shove. They were sitting on the floor, and the shove sent Happy into the coffee table. He banged his head on the corner.

"Look what you did," Happy said, holding his temple. "I'm bleeding."

"He's bleeding," everyone concurred, in unison. All except Grumpy, who glared defiantly at the circle of dwarfs, his arms crossed in front of him.

"Violence can't be tolerated," Doc said sternly.

"Oh, yeah? What are you gonna do about it?" Grumpy said. "You and your stupid Book. Nobody believes in that shit but you. They're all just humoring you, man."

"You're lying," Doc said. He looked around at the others. "He's lying, right?"

"Yeah, right," Sneezy said. "We believe."

"We believe," the others said. But it sounded wrong. Doc could hear the doubt in their voices, could see it in the way they shifted their eyes to the floor, hunching their shoulders. Bashful picked up his Big Mac in both hands and chewed, his head down.

"I absolutely, positively, believe," Sneezy said.

But Sneezy was a kid, Doc thought, who believed in dryads and unicorns, wizards and fairies, in Spiderman and Wolverine and other bullshit superheroes. Sneezy sat rapt in front of the Saturday morning cartoons, saying "Rad" and "Awesome." Sneezy's belief was not hard-won.

"Whatever gets you through," Dopey said, surprising everyone. Dopey never talked at house meetings. "It's cool," Dopey said. "She'll come, dudes." He lay back against the armrest of the couch and closed his eyes.

"It's just—" Bashful said.

"Just what," Doc said, his voice flat.

"We're kind of in a rut, I think. Maybe. Or something." Bashful stared at the hamburger in his hands. A little dribble of pink sauce was falling right onto the table Doc had cleaned.

"You have doubts," Doc said. "That's okay, that's perfectly natural."

But didn't Doc have his doubts, too? Didn't he lie awake at night, listening to the snores of the others, wondering if maybe she wasn't coming after all; didn't he try to bury those thoughts, to tell himself to be patient, to withstand the test of these long years? Some nights, when he couldn't sleep, he would get up and take the Book from the wooden lectern Bashful had built for it, and he would go into the bathroom and sit on the toilet lid and read it again. *Once upon a time. She ate the apple, she fell.* The dwarfs were there, in the story—they took care of her. The Book was a mess of half-pages, missing pages, the story erratic, interrupted. But some things were clear. A few powerful words shone forth, in large letters. There were faded illustrations that had once been bright: a man with an ax. A hand holding a huge, shining red apple. The stepmother and her mirror. But the page that might reveal *her*, that page was only a scrap, and all it showed was a short puffy white sleeve, and an inch of a pale arm, against which lay a heartbreaking curl of long, blue-black hair. So many mysteries, so many things they might never know. But in the end, on the very last page of the Book, the promise, the words that had given him such hope the first time he read them: *They lived happily ever after.* She and the dwarfs, Doc thought, all of them together. She would come and see that he had made things ready. She would take the pain that had always been with him, the great ache of loneliness at the center of his life, into her hands like a trembling bird; she would sing to it, and caress it, and then with one gesture fling it into the sky. A flutter of wings and it would rise away from him forever.

"They don't buy any of your religious mumbo-jumbo," Grumpy said. "They're just too chickenshit to tell you. Well,

I'm done, buddy boy. *Basta*." He lifted his chin and scratched his stubble, glaring at Doc.

"Grumpy," Sleepy said. "Don't go."

"And my name isn't Grumpy," Grumpy said. "It's Carlos. I'm a Puerto Rican"—he paused—"*little person*," he said. "I'm sick of all of you with your fake names and voodoo loser fantasies about some chick who ain't coming. She ain't coming, man. Get it through your fat heads."

No one looked at him. Grumpy stood up.

"All right then," he said. He went to the corner where he kept his sleeping bag and picked it up. "*Adiós*, you chumps. See you around."

Doc listened to his boots on the stairs. It doesn't matter, he told himself. It doesn't matter. She'll still come.

"A dwarf by any other name—" Happy said.

"Would still be an asshole," Sleepy said.

"My name used to be Steven," Sneezy said, and Sleepy told him to shut his fucking piehole.

• • •

It was a Friday afternoon in November, full of wind and rain, and everyone who came into Oz shook out their umbrellas and dripped water onto the yellow brick tiles in the foyer, and asked for one of the tables close to the big stone fireplace.

Doc was short-staffed. A waiter was out with the flu, and Bashful had left town on Tuesday to attend an aunt's funeral. On Thursday, he had called to say he might not be coming back, except to pick up a few of his things.

"Of course you're coming back," Doc had said.

"She left me some money," Bashful said. "Nobody thought she had any. She lived in this crummy little studio apartment and never bought a thing. Turns out she had stocks from my grandfather, and she left it all to me and her cat. I'm the trustee for the cat."

"You can't just take off."

"I want to live there for a while. See how things go. I'm sorry, Doc. This just seems like the right thing for me now."

A couple of men came into the restaurant, dressed in matching red parkas, their arms around each other. The first man's hair was blond and combed back off a perfectly proportioned face; the other man had a square jaw, a neatly trimmed black beard, and when he shucked his parka Doc saw his chest and biceps outlined in a tight thermal shirt.

"Nasty weather out there," Doc said. He stepped down from his stool behind the podium to lead them to a table near the fireplace. He heard one man whisper something to the other, and the second's "Shh, he'll hear you." He was used to comments. On the street, teenagers yelled to him from passing cars. People stared, or else tried not to, averting their eyes and then casting furtive glances in his direction. Children walked right up to him, fascinated that he was their size, but different. He'd learned to block it out. But when the men were seated he walked away from them, feeling a sudden, overwhelming rage.

Things were falling apart at home. At night he would sit on the couch, the Book on his lap, and read a few sentences aloud. In the old days, everyone would gather around, relaxing with cigarettes and beers, and maybe some dessert they'd brought back from the restaurant. But now they drifted away. To the kitchen, or up to the loft to turn on the TV and watch some inane show he could hear as he tried to focus on the words in the Book, the all-important words that were going to change their lives. That had changed Doc's life, given him hope. But now that hope was being drained away. One by one they were going to leave him. And she would never come, not to a lone dwarf. An old, balding dwarf whose feet and back hurt him every night so that he had to soak in a hot bath for some relief. She wouldn't take his gnarled, aching feet in her hands and massage them. In the black nights when he lay awake and empty, she wouldn't lay her long white body, smelling of apples, on top of his.

As the evening went on he forced himself to greet customers pleasantly, not to yell at Sleepy when he dropped a bus tray, or at Happy when he mixed up orders—Happy was filling in tonight for the absent waiter. Doc focused on keeping everything running smoothly, not letting it get chaotic. He let a German woman pull him onto her lap so her friends could take a picture with their cell phones, beaming the image to other friends in Stuttgart. He sang "Happy Birthday" with the other dwarfs and handed a giant lollipop to a girl with a magenta buzz cut and several facial piercings, while her parents sat there with strained smiles on their faces, obviously uncomfortable that they found themselves with such a weird-looking daughter and were now confronted with several pseudo-Munchkins in striped tights. By closing time he wanted to hit something. He took his time totaling up the evening's receipts, to give everyone a chance to finish up in the kitchen and leave him alone. Finally, Sleepy, Happy, and Sneezy appeared and hovered around the office door.

"Just go," Doc said.

"What's the matter?" Happy said. "Is it me? I did my best. It's hard being a waiter. I never realized it was so hard, keeping everything straight."

"You did fine," Doc said.

"Do you really think so?" Happy looked thrilled.

"We'll wait for you," Sleepy said. "We can all share a cab."

"You guys go," Doc said.

"Cool, a cab," Sneezy said. "Here's something weird," he said. "Whenever I get in somebody's car, I make sure to buckle up. But in a cab, I never put on a seat belt. Isn't that weird?"

"You should," Doc said. He wanted to slap them. "Go," he said. "Just get the fuck out of here and leave me alone."

Sneezy and Happy stared. Sleepy pulled them each by a jacket sleeve. "Sure, man," Sleepy said. "No problem. You want to be alone, we'll leave you alone."

Finally they were gone. "Over the Rainbow" was playing softly on the stereo. Judy Garland's voice usually soothed him, but now Doc felt mocked by the promise in the song, the sappy land where dreams came true, the bluebirds and the bright colors everywhere, troubles melting away.

He locked the zippered bag of credit card slips and money into the safe. He switched off the stereo and straightened the stack of CDs beside it, then turned off the last of the lights. The alarm code had to be set by punching numbers into a keypad by the door that led from the kitchen to the alley; he was about to set it, but stopped. He walked back through the dark kitchen, out the swinging doors into the restaurant and behind the bar, and took a bottle of Johnny Walker and a rocks glass.

. . .

At four a.m. the streets in this part of the city looked like a movie set about to be struck. The storefront businesses had mostly failed. Lights shone in the tall office buildings, where janitors were emptying wastebaskets and running vacuum cleaners. Doc knew what that was like; he'd done it, years ago, a flask in his back pocket that he'd drink from through the night, working under the fluorescent glare while everyone else slept. At dawn he'd be ready to pass out, and would reel off to find a hospitable bench or doorway. He'd forgotten the feeling of drunkenness, the happy, buzzy glow, how the world shifted pleasantly out of focus and retreated to a manageable distance. He staggered in the direction of the loft, clutching the bottle to his coat, hardly feeling the rain that was still falling, though not with its earlier force. Now it was soft, almost a mist, cold kisses on the top of his bare head, a damp chill coming up through his shoes.

He sang "Brown-Eyed Girl" and "Swanee River." He stopped in the middle of the street and looked around to see if anyone had heard him, but no one was there. A cat slid away, around the corner of a building, pale against the dark bricks. He was breathing kind of hard, he realized. He stopped to rest in a small park, a square of grass with a single wrought-iron bench, a narrow border of dirt—mud, now—where there were white flowers in spring. He remembered the flowers and looked sadly at the wet soil. No flowers. There would never be flowers again.

It was never going to stop raining. The rain would wash away the soil, and the park, and himself; he would float down the river of rain, endlessly, until he sank beneath the surface of the water, down to the bottom like a rock, dead and inert, and finally at peace. He looked for his glass, to pour himself more liquor, but he had lost it somewhere. He had a vague memory of seeing it smash against bricks, the pieces glittering like the rain, lying under a streetlight. He took a pull from the bottle and slumped against the freezing iron of the bench.

His dreams were confused: having his picture taken with tourists at the restaurant, only the restaurant was really an office building and their meals were being served on desks, and water was seeping through the carpet and he was down on his knees trying to find where it was coming from. When he woke he was lying on the wet grass, under a dripping tree. The rain had let up. It was getting light; the air was slate-colored. He was still slightly drunk, and he could feel underneath the cushion of alcohol the hard, unyielding bedrock of a massive hangover. He got up and walked over to the bench, where the bottle was lying tucked under a newspaper like a tiny version of a homeless man. He picked up both and laid them gently in the wire trash receptacle next to the bench.

On the way home he passed a few actual homeless people, still asleep in doorways. He peered at each of them, but none of them was Grumpy. There was one dog, black and scrawny, that raised its head as Doc passed and then settled, sighing, next to its master.

He let himself into the building and trudged upstairs, stopping on each landing to catch his breath and stop the grinding in his head. He opened the door to the loft quietly, in case anyone was up. But it was too early. He could hear the steady snores of Happy and Sleepy, and Sneezy's asthmatic breathing. Dopey slept alone in the double bed, angled across it, one arm dangling out from the covers. Beside the bed were an overflowing ashtray, a box of wooden matches, and a litter of pistachio shells. Doc knelt down and scooped up the shells and threw them away in the kitchen. He went back and got the ashtray and matches, emptied the ashtray, and put the box of matches on the shelf where they belonged. He rinsed a few dishes that were in the sink and set them in the dishwasher, then tidied up the counter—someone had apparently consumed a late-night snack of cereal and pretzels.

Someone had also brought home flowers. There were irises in a vase—a vase stolen from the restaurant, Doc noted—set on a cleared section of the counter. Around the main room were stalks of star lilies in quart beer bottles. On the coffee table, which had been cleaned off, was a Pyrex bowl of fruit— oranges and grapefruits and apples and a bunch of bananas— flanked by two candles that had burned down to stumps. Also on the table was a homemade card, featuring a drawing that looked like Sneezy's work. It was a pretty good likeness of Doc, and on the inside, in Happy's loopy script, *We Love You, Doc* was written in blue across the yellow construction paper.

Doc took an apple and went to the row of windows. A few cars crawled by below, the first trickle of morning commuters, their headlights still on. Clouds hung over the city, pearl smudges above gray buildings. There wasn't any glorious shaft of sunlight breaking through to set the thousands of windows glittering, or any rainbow arcing over the dense trees of the park at the far end of the city. There was no black-haired goddess, eyes dark and full of love, floating toward him. He polished the apple on his shirt. His was a small life. His head was barely higher than the window sill, but he could see that out there, in the big world, there was nothing anymore to wish for.

INTUITION

When I see the boy at the movies, standing behind the candy counter in his striped shirt and paper hat, I know we'll be together. Not consciously, of course—it's all my intuition. Intuition is about the unconscious, which is a murky weird place where shit happens that you'll never begin to understand. It's like a deep hole in outer space. Only it's not cold and dead like it might sound. It's like a tropical jungle, too, with things slithering down from branches and nosing through greenish water and running fast through the leaves. I watch the boy hand an overflowing tub of popcorn to a man with a violent twitch, then clean the spilled popcorn off the counter with a flip of his rag. He turns from the soda machine with two big Diet Cokes for me and Heather, his dark curls corkscrewing to his jawline. I see how he flicks his eyes over Heather and looks at me a fraction of a second longer.

"Here ya go, girls," he says.

Him, I think.

The cups are identical, big and red with plastic lids and straws poked through the lids. He takes the money Heather hands him without looking at either of us, does a little half-turn toward the register, rings up the purchase, counts out the change, and slams the drawer shut with the heel of his hand. I'm watching him and he knows it. Heather, stupid cow, is completely oblivious. She doesn't ever listen to her intuition. I know, because her so-called intuition says things like *We should really go now* and *Don't, Faith, we'll get in trouble*.

"That boy was hot," I whisper to Heather as we hit the dark of the theater and stop for a second to orient ourselves. The previews have already started. We make our way down and have to sit in the third row, because it's Saturday night and crowded. I take a quick look back after we get our seats and see groups of girls, but also plenty of couples, and I wish I had somebody besides Heather to sit with.

Most of my Saturday nights are spent with Heather. My Friday nights, too. Also, okay, lunches at school. So I'm not an It Girl. I wear all black, in a high school swarming with pastels. My hair is short and spiky, while the other girls wear theirs long. Those girls have pierced ears, but I have a hole in the middle of my tongue and a steel ball that clicks against my teeth. In San Francisco, where I plan to live when I'm done with school, I am going to fit right in, but right here, right now, I am the most bizarre thing going.

As soon as the feature starts, Heather pulls out a big package of Red Vines from her purse and starts chewing. Heather is fat and looks very bovine when she eats.

"Don't chew so loud," I say. "It's disgusting."

"Sorry," she says.

"You embarrass me."

"Oh, Faith, no one's looking." She pulls another drooping licorice vine from the package with a loud crinkling of the plastic.

"Jesus, Heather!" I say. I pinch her on the inside of her upper arm and she flinches, but doesn't squeal.

"I'm sorry," she says. She sinks in her seat until her chin rests on her chest and sticks the candy in her mouth.

The movie is the usual lies. The boy is really sensitive, and really loves the girl, and they get it all worked out after a bunch of crap gets in their way. Maybe some of the boys sitting behind us with their dates are actually like that, nice boys who have real feelings. None of them go to our school, that's for sure. The boys at our school are cruel. They say things right to your face: *Weirdo. Lezzie.* They moo when Heather goes by. I would never do that, even though I think it sometimes: *Moooooo, Heather, you are so dumb and pathetic I can't believe you're my friend.* I've known her since elementary school, though, so she's more like a sister who I put up with. She used to be a grade ahead of me, but I skipped the ninth grade and went straight to sophomore year. Now, we're both juniors, but I'm taking senior math. I'm outgrowing her, is what I'm saying. My intuition tells me I'm headed for better things.

I sit through the movie tingling and wondering how to strike up a conversation with the boy behind the counter, and in the middle of a sappy love scene with the camera circling around the two perfect lip-locked teenagers, I tell Heather I have to pee and go out to the lobby. There are people in line for snacks because some other movie is starting, so I get behind them and wait.

When I get to the counter I let my intuition lead me.

"Hey," I say.

"Hey," the boy says. "More Diet Coke?"

"You remembered."

He doesn't say anything, just leans on his hands on the counter and looks at me. I look at his hands, at a white scar below one knuckle and a long scrape on his forearm that's healing and scabbing.

"We were thinking maybe we could use something stronger, after," I say. "But we're too young to buy." I know he's too young to buy liquor, too, but I figure he has some way—a fake ID, an older friend or sister, parents who don't keep track.

"I can get you something," he says. "You girls want to wait for me when I'm done? I'm off at eleven-thirty."

"Sure," I say. "I better get back to my friend. Her name's Heather."

I wait, but he doesn't ask mine.

"Later," he says.

• • •

The boy from the movies is named Jim. He brought us to this big house with a wraparound porch, where a massive party is happening, and then disappeared into the crowd. Heather and I are sitting on a small futon couch that Heather takes up nearly half of. No one's paying any attention to her. A tiny blonde girl sitting cross-legged on the floor is telling a long, complicated story about partying with some rock band in a hotel room downtown, and a half-dozen people are listening to her like she's a rock star herself.

"Me and a bunch of the other girls ended up having a rainbow party with him," the girl says.

"With Petey?" someone says. "No fucking way."

"ROY G. BIV," someone says, like it's grade school and everybody needs to remember the color spectrum. Everybody laughs. I laugh, too, but I don't know what a rainbow party is or why what she said was funny.

"What band is that again?" I say. I've started sweating like crazy. I can feel the dampness under my armpits, and I squeeze my arms close to my body in case it shows.

The girl who was talking looks at me.

"The Losers," she says.

Everybody laughs again, and the girl flashes them all a brilliant smile.

"I'm going outside to have a cigarette," I tell Heather.

"I'll go with you." She starts to get up, but I push her shoulders down.

"No, you stay here. Quit following me everywhere like a baby."

"But I don't know anybody here, Faith." She looks around fearfully from under her long hair. She actually has kind of a pretty face, when you can catch a glimpse of it.

"Stay," I tell her. "I'll be right back."

I go down the steps, past a group of people on the porch singing "Benny and the Jets" at the top of their lungs, and crunch along the gravel driveway. Near the end of the driveway I find a big tree and stand in its shadow to light a cigarette. I'm on my second when Jim comes out carrying a bottle of Wild Turkey.

"Yo," he says. "Look what I scored from the kitchen. Let's head."

I follow him to his car, a big boat of a car with some fraying rope holding the bumper on. I look back at the house, all lit up like something burning, loud music thumping inside. I think about Heather, getting up to look for me, panicking when she can't find me.

"Maybe I should stay," I say.

Jim shrugs. "Whatever."

I turn toward the house, then stop. I feel bad about Heather, but it's like I can't help myself. My intuition tells me it's now or never with Jim, so I turn back and get in the car. In another minute the house is gone, behind us. The car rattles along; it needs shocks. Every time we hit a rough patch of road I spill some of the Wild Turkey we're passing back and forth. I'm kind of glad because I figure I'll smell like liquor and not so much like my sweat.

• • •

On the phone, Heather says, "I hate you, Faith."

"I meant to make it back to the party to find you. I swear I did."

"Shit, Faith. I didn't even know where I was. I had to call my dad to come and get me."

"Did my mom call your house?" I say.

I was supposed to be sleeping over at Heather's last night. Instead, I slept in Jim's bed, next to Jim, under a poster of

164

Spiderman crouching on top of a skyscraper in some moody, blue and black city. In the middle of the night he rolled over and accidentally laid his arm across me. The crook of his elbow fell across my waist. I felt it and woke up, and then I didn't really sleep. I lay looking at a water heater against the opposite wall and at a little mesh window up near the ceiling where light from the street was coming in. I looked at Jim's hand on the sheet and imagined Jim and me in love, like the couple in the movie earlier, eating at fancy restaurants and walking through parks with fountains and stopping to kiss in the middle of a hotel lobby while the world spins around us. Then we would go to our fancy hotel room and take a bath together, Jim leaning back against my naked breasts while I worked a lather of shampoo into his dark curls. I knew it was crap, but I thought about it anyway.

The thing is, you keep hoping. With each boy, you think maybe it will happen: he'll look a you at certain way, he'll *get* you, and your search will be over. I've been searching since I was thirteen, with one boy after another.

I've been disappointed too many times to count.

This morning, Jim and I did it one more time, and he kept his eyes closed. I knew he was watching some movie in his head, and it wasn't the one I'd been imagining all night, with the two of us in the fancy hotel. I knew it was probably porno, some girl with long blonde hair bent over a desk in a cheesy office. I told myself it didn't matter. I moaned really loud, like I was into it, and hated him.

When he drove me to the end of my street to drop me off, he didn't ask for my number.

"So, bye, I guess," I said, my hand on the door handle.

"See you around," he said, eyes straight ahead, fingers tapping the steering wheel.

"I'm not going to lie for you," Heather says now. "But no, your mom didn't call. Lucky for you."

My mom almost never calls; she's used to me spending time at Heather's house. Every once in a while, though, out of the blue, she remembers she has a daughter and picks up the phone. She works long hours for the Public Utilities Commission—which she says is a cesspool of politics and corruption, the blind leading the stupid—and she's getting her real estate license at night. My dad has been out of the picture for three years. Every year he sends a lame card for my birthday that usually comes about a week late, because my mom has had to call and remind him. This year the card said, *So You're Sweet Sixteen*, even though I was turning fifteen. The card was signed, *Love, Dad*, in his new wife's handwriting, and there was a check for a hundred dollars, signed by him. The last time I saw him was right after the divorce, when I had my eleventh birthday party at Chuck E. Cheese; he stopped by with his new wife and baby and dropped off a plush animal, a German Shepherd bigger than I was. I put it in the garbage can the next day.

"You're right," I say. "I *am* lucky. I get boys all the time. You never get lucky."

"That's mean," Heather says.

"If you tell my mom anything," I say, "I'll cut you."

"For sure," Heather says. "Like you would."

"I'm sorry about ditching you."

"No, you're not. You always say that, but you just go and do it again."

"You'd do the same thing," I say.

"No, I wouldn't."

But my intuition tells me otherwise.

"Yes," I say. "You would."

"I'm not a slut, like you. I want a boy who respects me."

I don't know what to say to that, so I hang up on her.

• • •

Heather and I are at the 31 Flavors, deciding. Or rather, she's deciding, taking forever to choose between mocha chip and Cookies 'n Cream and about five other flavors. I always just walk up, look into the tubs, and pick whatever calls to me first, usually something chocolate.

Heather and I made up after a few days of ignoring each other at school, sitting alone at lunch. Sitting alone is the worst. At the other tables, and sometimes at the other end of yours, kids are talking and laughing. You look down at your brown cafeteria tray and crummy food and pretend to be really interested in it, or in looking over your Earth Science notes, and you feel like everybody's staring at you. The worst part is, they aren't. Most of the time they don't even know you're alive. And when they do, you'd rather they forgot about you again.

"Can I taste the mint chip?" Heather says, looking intently through the glass at the ice cream, like it's a life or death decision. This is the third taste she's asked for. The boy behind the counter sighs, then goes and gets another teeny pink plastic spoon and dips it in and hands it to her. He's tall and skinny and his hair is tied back in a greasy ponytail, and he doesn't look at me twice.

Which is fine with me, except that he's looking at Heather.

"Hey," he says. "Algebra, right?"

Heather sucks on the spoon, which looks even teenier in her fat hand. "Uh-huh," she says. "Okay, I'll take, um—I guess the, uh—. Oh, you pick," she says.

"You want the mint chip?" the boy says.

"That's fine," she says. She smiles at him. "Algebra is boring," she says.

"Yeah, it sucks big time," he says, smiling back.

I am not believing what I see here.

"Wait until you get to Trig," I say loudly. "Trig really sucks."

The boy is busy scooping, and doesn't answer me. Heather gives me a look that says, *Cut it out.*

The boy straightens up and hands Heather her cone. Sugar, of course.

"Did you figure out the homework?" the boy says, pushing a fallen strand of his greasy hair from his greasy face. There is a pimple on his chin, like a red chip in vanilla ice cream.

"Pretty much," Heather says. "Except for the last word problem."

"Bob's father is three times as old as Bob," the boy says. "Four years ago he was four times older."

"Like, who cares how old Bob's father is?" Heather says.

"If x is Bob and y is his father," the boy says, "then 3x equals y."

"That's as far as I got," she says. "I couldn't figure out what to do after that."

"It was a bitch," the boy agrees.

You're a bitch, Heather, I'm thinking. They go on discussing the stupid algebra problem, and I tune out. I mean, like, duh. Bob's father is thirty-three. I go sit on a molded pink plastic chair and stick my legs out in front of me and eat my ice cream as fast as I can. I reach into my purse and feel my Buck knife, nestled next to my wallet, and rub my thumb along the place it clicks open. I bought it at a store downtown that had a whole case of knives. The man who sold it to me showed me how to open and close it safely, and also explained how to hand an open knife to someone else so it doesn't hurt them. I have it for protection, because you never know. A girl in our school went out jogging by the lake last summer and her nude body was found ten miles away at the landfill.

Heather laughs and I want to hit her. I close my eyes and think about Jim. Both his nipples were pierced with little silver rings. He told me what a rainbow party is: a bunch of girls get together, put on different colors of lipstick, and make a rainbow on a certain part of the boy's body.

"Did that ever happen to you?" I asked.

"I should be so lucky," he said.

I think about him putting on the condom, pushing in between my thighs. Except for telling me about the rainbow party, he hardly said anything to me except *Turn over* and *Yeah, yeah* and *I think I'm done* after he came. So my intuition says, forget Jim. Find someone new.

"Heather," I say. "Let's go."

She turns toward me and I see her face change. One minute it's all lit up and happy, and the next it's the usual drooping cow eyes and downturned mouth. "I need a cigarette," I say. "Come on." I get up and walk out without looking back.

• • •

It's another thrilling Saturday night with Heather. We made chocolate chip cookies. Heather's had about ten so far, sitting on her basement couch in her pajamas with the little hearts all over them. I've got on a blue nightgown with a little pocket on it and an anchor stitched on the pocket. We're watching a chick flick we rented, about a girl who starts out supposedly ugly, who the cutest boy in school is dared to date. You can tell she isn't really ugly, though. They put glasses on her and had her hunch over and wear baggy clothes, but you can tell she's as beautiful as the rest of them.

"I'm going to get more cookies," I say. "Want more milk?"

"Yeah," she says. "Thanks."

"Moo," I say. It just slips out.

She looks at me, but doesn't say anything. She crosses her arms over her chest and turns back to the movie. The girl in the movie has taken off her glasses and, surprise, she looks gorgeous.

I go upstairs and into the big kitchen, which has a hardwood floor. It used to be red and white linoleum, before Heather's parents remodeled a few years ago. There's a red armchair in one corner that's been there since I was eight or nine, and a little rug and lamp, and there's another rug in front of the big butcher block counter in the center. I like Heather's house better than mine. It's messy and cozy and looks like somebody lives in it. Mine looks like it was furnished by the same people that supply stuff for Best Westerns or Holiday Inns. Everything is hideous and matches everything else. I open the fridge and stand there, enjoying the cold exhalation of air that washes over me.

Heather's dad comes into the kitchen in his bathrobe, followed by their old dog, a fat beagle named Fred. I remember when Fred was a squirmy little puppy, and how I used to pretend he was mine. Fred's nails go click, click, click on the floor.

"You girls having a good night?" he says.

"I guess. We made some cookies."

Fred goes over to his smelly plaid bed by the stove and plops into it with a sigh. When he was a puppy, he used to sleep with me and Heather, on the end of her bed. Now he's not allowed to sleep anywhere but the kitchen, because he pees himself sometimes in the middle of the night.

"You look cold, honey," he says. "You should put something else on."

I look down and see that my nipples are kind of sticking out. *Smuggling raisins*, I heard a girl at school say once. *A tit nipply*, she said, and the girls with her laughed. Those are the girls that usually pretend they don't see you, that walk right past you like you're dead air.

I look at Heather's dad. He's got gray in his hair, and he's kind of big-boned, like Heather, but he's not fat. I've seen him with his shirt off riding the mower around their yard. His chest hair is still dark. He used to let me ride on his lap on the mower, but he hasn't done that in a few years. I've been in love with him forever. I used to think he loved me back, but now I don't know. A couple of years ago he walked in on me when

I was changing, when Heather was in the bathroom down the hall. He stood in the doorway, looking at me. I had my jeans on but no shirt, and I automatically covered my breasts. They were hardly there yet, just starting to develop. But then I let my hands fall to my sides. We stood there a minute, and then he lowered his eyes and backed out. Since then, he always seems to be avoiding me; when I hug him, he acts all weird, going, *Okay, enough,* as soon as I put my arms around him. I mean, I've been hugging him practically my whole life, so I don't know what his problem is.

I lean into the fridge and pull out the square Tupperware full of cookies. I left one batch in the oven for too long, so a few of them are a little overdone on the bottom. For a second I feel like crying because they didn't all come out perfect. It's Heather's fault, I know, but I feel like it's mine. She was supposed to watch that batch while I had a cigarette on the back porch, but she ran to call the pimply Baskin Robbins boy instead. I push the browner cookies under the tan ones and take them over to Heather's dad.

"Do you want some? There's plenty."

"Yeah," he says.

"I knew it," I say. "Got the munchies?" Heather's dad is a pothead. He works at a Honda dealership, and he once told me that getting stoned is the only thing that gets him through the day. Heather and I sometimes steal joints from his stash.

"Don't tell Leslie or she'll kill me," he said. Leslie is Mrs. Phillips. I don't like hearing her name like that, like she's his girlfriend.

"Thanks," he says, picking up a cookie.

"Hey," I say. "How come you don't like me to hug you anymore?"

"What?" he says.

"You act like I'm diseased or something."

"I'm sorry," he says.

"Can I smoke some pot with you?"

He looks around, like Mrs. Phillips might appear any minute, but she's not even home. "Okay," he says. "Let's go out on the porch."

We sit side by side on the two-person swing that glides back and forth, and when he goes to light the joint I lean my head against his shoulder, like I did when I was little. We pass the joint a couple of times, and then I let my hand move over to his thigh.

"Hey, cut it out," he says. He doesn't get up, though.

I walk my fingers along his leg and up his chest, playing eensy-weensy spider.

"Down came the rain," I say, and when I get to the part about going up the spout again, I walk my fingers right over to the place between his legs, where he's already hard, and he settles back and opens them a little.

• • •

My mom wants to know why I'm spending all my time at Heather's house these days. She doesn't see why I have to stay over there every weekend, why I never have Heather over to our house anymore.

"It's a project for school," I say. "We have to do it at her house."

My mom doesn't ask what kind of project. She just says,

"Okay," and goes back to doing her real estate homework at the dining room table, which we never use for dining. My mom lately is all about voluntary and involuntary liens. Appraisals. Escrow and title insurance. She couldn't care less about what I'm up to. If she had any intuition at all, car alarms would be going off in her head. But she doesn't have a clue.

Heather's dad is three times as old as me. When I turn thirty, he will be only twice as old as me.

Heather's dad, who I used to call Mr. Phillips or sir—as in, Hi Mr. Phillips, or Thank you for driving us, sir—now I call him Barry. Not when Heather or her mom are around, but when he and I are alone. I sneak out of Heather's room at night and tiptoe down the carpeted stairs in my blue night-gown, stopping on the main floor to slip off my underwear and ball it in my hand, and then Barry and I make love on the couch in the basement where Heather and I watched TV earlier. Or I hop the bus downtown after school, and he takes me to the Dairy Queen off the interstate for a Pecan Mud-slide and then to the Tip Top Motel. We always get room 7, if it's available. It's on the second floor, around back, and has a view of a parking lot and a dental office if you open the gold curtains, which we never do. We keep them closed, and turn on the two lamps by the bed and the light on the far wall, and Barry picks a movie from Adult Pleasures on the TV menu.

Men are different from boys. They have true confidence and not just bravado. They make you feel that way, too. They pay for things and open doors and tell you you're beautiful. They tell you what to do, but not in a mean way.

"When I'm sixty, you'll be the sum of my age plus one-half my age," I tell Barry.

"Age is a state of mind," he says, passing me the joint he's rolled. We're sitting in his Honda in a far corner of the mall parking lot, the windows rolled up. Closer to the building there's a sea of cars, but where we are it's all white diagonal lines across empty asphalt.

"When I'm ninety," I say, taking a hit, "you'll be my age plus a third."

"When you're ninety, I'll be dead," he says.

"As we approached infinity, the distance between us would grow smaller."

"Not really. There's a thing about infinity. I'm trying to remember. What the fuck is it? Something about points on a line." The smoke wreathes around the car. He closes his eyes.

"In relative terms, I mean. Like, when I'm three hundred, you'll be—"

"Enough, already!" he says, his eyes still closed.

"Sorry."

"You think too much," Barry says. "You should enjoy being young. Fuck, I wish I was sixteen again."

"I'm fifteen," I remind him.

I stare at the mall through the windshield. I never noticed how ugly malls are on the outside—big boxes with fading paint and a few lame bushes. Inside they're all nice lighting and flowers and fountains and inviting stores, but from this vantage point they're nothing.

"I thought you said I was mature," I say.

"You are, babe." He puts his arm across the back of my seat.

"Most girls your age don't know what they want. They want sex, but they're afraid of it."

"I rely a lot on my intuition," I say.

I watch people getting out of their cars, going in and out of the glass doors that lead to the cineplex and then the food court and then all the bright stores. From here they look small and far away. I feel like we're alone in the world, Barry and I, but not lonely.

"See? A woman's intuition. Better than thinking any day of the week." He puts his hand against the back of my head, stroking my hair.

• • •

Heather and I are sitting in the courtyard off the school cafeteria, at our usual table. It's Friday afternoon, so the courtyard isn't crowded. Now that it's spring, most of the seniors take off at lunch on Fridays and don't come back. They go to a park by the river and get drunk and throw Frisbees. Next year, when Heather and I are seniors, I bet we'll still be sitting here.

"You can't come over tonight," Heather says.

"Why not? You have a big date or something?"

"Yes," she says, icicles dripping from her voice. "I have a date."

A few white blossoms are shaking loose from the trees in the wind, so it seems like it's snowing. Heather is pushing her fat, crinkle-cut french fries around on her plate, not looking at me.

"Like I care," I say.

"Like you don't," she says.

"Is it that zit-faced guy from 31 Flavors?"

"You have a zit right now," Heather points out. "We're going to the movies," she says.

I touch my face self-consciously. I've been putting Persa-Gel on it for two days, but it hasn't done a thing.

"Can I come with you guys?"

She looks at me then. "No," she says. She stands up and picks up her tray, even though her hamburger is only half-finished. She's been doing that lately, just picking at her food and throwing most of it away. It's something I taught her. It's working, too. She probably looks the same to everyone else, but I can tell she's lost five pounds, at least.

"Well," I say, "what if I just go hang at your house? I'll stay in your room. Then you can tell me about your date when you get back."

She stands there, thinking it over. I look up at her; the sun's glaring behind her so she's kind of hard to see. For a minute I'm afraid she's going to say no, and I won't get to sneak downstairs late at night to be with Barry. I'll have to stay at my own house, where there's nothing to do, where my mom will be at the dining room table drinking endless cups of Earl Gray tea and reading *Fundamentals of Real Estate Appraisal*. I'll be leaning out my bedroom window, taking drags off a cigarette, putting the butts in a Diet Coke can. I'll be going down the hall to the bathroom and running scalding water on my hands just to feel like I exist.

"Okay," Heather says. "Come over around six and you can have dinner with me and my parents. My mom has a meeting, anyway."

I wonder how long Heather's mom will be at AA. "Your dad won't mind?" I say.

She shrugs and goes to dump her tray.

I eat all the food on my plate, then open my purse and pretend to be looking for something in it. I put my hand on my knife, flipping it open and closed inside my purse. I imagine following Heather and her pimply boyfriend into the movies, sitting behind them in the dark. He's slipped his arm over her shoulder. When she gets up and goes for the free popcorn refill, I lean forward, hook my arm around him, and put the blade to his scrawny throat. It scares him, and by the time Heather gets back with the popcorn there's an empty seat where he was. I imagine Heather crying like a little baby, thinking that he ditched her, then coming back to her house and finding me in her room, painting my toenails with glittery polish. *Darling*, I'll say, patting the bed beside me. *Come and tell me all about it. Boys are such pigs*, I'll say.

· · ·

Heather doesn't get back from the movies until late. I didn't get to be with Barry yet, because Mrs. Phillips decided not to go to her AA meeting. I waited in Heather's room, listening for Mrs. Phillips's car pulling out of the driveway, but it stayed put. At dinner she gave me a strange look, and I wondered if she knew what her husband and I had been up to for the past few weeks, but then she smiled at me and asked if my mom had gotten her license yet.

"She's still studying for the exam."

"I'm sure she'll do very well," Mrs. Phillips said. "Real estate is an excellent field, isn't it, Barry?"

"No kidding," he said. "The property values around here are skyrocketing."

"Lucky we bought when we did."

I acted as normal as I could, but I felt weird. I knocked over my glass of milk and just stared at it, paralyzed for a second, while the milk seeped into the cloth placemat. Barry seemed weird, too. He wouldn't meet my eyes. He didn't joke with me the way he used to when I came for dinner, calling me Faithy and asking me if I still got straight As in school, or if I'd slipped yet and gotten a B. I was afraid I was going to say something to blow it, and then I wanted to. *Mrs. Phillips,* I wanted to say. *Don't you know anything? Don't you know how Barry and I feel about each other?*

"Pie?" Mrs. Phillips said, and passed it to me with a plastic spatula. I love her peach pie. I lifted out a big piece and set it on my plate.

"I don't think we could afford this house if it were on the market today, do you, hon?" she said to Barry.

At the word *hon,* I dropped my fork on the floor.

Now Heather is coming into her room where I'm stretched out on her four-poster bed smoking a cigarette, blowing the smoke up toward the white, ruffled canopy.

"Don't!" she screams. "What is *wrong* with you! My parents will kill me."

"The window's wide open," I say. "They won't smell anything."

She comes over and snatches the cigarette from me. "This is *my* house," she says.

"How was your date?" I say. "What took you so long?"

She sits on the end of the bed. "We went and watched the skateboarders at the bank plaza downtown. Then we played some video games. Then we went to 31 Flavors and got free ice cream."

She bounces up and down on the bed. "I like him, Faith," she says.

"That's great," I say, thinking, *I'd like to tell you about my dates with your father. About room 7 at the Tip Top, and being on my hands and knees on the diamond-patterned carpet wearing nothing but the high heels your father bought me. About the sounds of the porn movie and your father's groans. I'd like to tell you what it's like to be a woman, to make love with a real man. You clueless cow,* I'm thinking.

"We saw that guy Jim from the movies," she says. "Skateboarding. He's really good."

"Oh," I say. I haven't thought about Jim for a while now. Barry made me forget all about Jim with his curly hair and pierced nipples, Jim dropping me off and racing away in his car.

"He had a real crowd around him," Heather says.

"So," I say. "Who cares."

"He had a girlfriend, too. We ran into them at 31 Flavors. He remembered me. Funny, he didn't ask about you."

"Fuck you, Heather."

"What?" she says. "I'm just telling you about my night. What did you do?"

"Not a thing."

I only left Heather's room once. I went downstairs to the kitchen, to sneak another piece of pie. When I got to the doorway, I saw Mrs. Phillips sitting at the table in the breakfast nook in a terrycloth robe, her back to me. She had her hand around a frosty glass that might have been cold water from the built-in ice and water dispenser on their refrigerator. It might have been something else, though. Fred was lying across her bare feet, and when he saw me, he thumped his tail on the floor and started to get up, and I came back upstairs.

"I'm going to sleep now," I tell Heather.

"Go ahead," she says. "He likes me," she says.

．　．　．

The digital alarm clock by Heather's bed says 3:17 a.m. I wake up every night around this time now, whether I'm sneaking off to see Barry or not. At home I get up and smoke a cigarette by my window, looking out at the boring houses in my neighborhood. I usually can't get back to sleep for a couple of hours. It's a bad time of night and I miss Barry terribly if I can't see him.

Heather is rolled over on her side, facing away from me. I slide out of bed and quietly pick up my purse from the floor because I want to go have a smoke on their back porch. Sometimes that's where Barry finds me; he'll take my cigarette for himself, even though he pretty much quit years ago. He'll sit next to me on the swing, and I'll lay my head against his shoulder while he smokes, and he'll stroke my hair or my breast, and take my nipple between his thumb and forefinger and squeeze it a little.

I go downstairs and unlock the door that leads to the porch. I sit on the swing and smoke. The Phillipses' backyard is gray in the moonlight. There's a picnic table, a gas barbecue, a couple of plastic chaise lounges. Above the fence is the second story of another house, all the windows dark. Everything looks ordinary and familiar. By the oak near the fence, I know, there's a little circle of white rocks marking where Heather and I buried her old cat, Missy, years ago. Next to the rosebushes is where we found a shell necklace I lost. I know every inch of this yard by heart.

"Hey," Barry says quietly, stepping out on the porch in his pajamas and bare feet.

My heart starts to thump and I think of Fred's tail on the wooden floor. It's been three days since I've been with Barry, and that seems like a really long time.

He sits next to me, like always, and takes my cigarette from me. He leans back, but he doesn't put his arm around me.

"Faith," he says.

I nuzzle my face into his chest and put my ear against his heart, which is slow and steady. His cologne smells sharp, the way it does when he's just put it on. I breathe in, and close my eyes.

"This has got to stop," he says.

My own heart freezes then. I sit up abruptly, and the swing shudders a little on its chains. "No," I say, not looking at him. "No, it doesn't."

"I'm married," he says. "I'm too old for you."

I think: Heather's dad is three times as old as Faith. Five years ago, he was four times older. How old is Heather's dad?

He goes on talking. I listen to what he's saying, to all the reasons we shouldn't be together, but something tells me he's lying. All those reasons were there before, and they didn't stop him from being with me. There's something else. It takes me another minute to figure it out, and then I get it.

In word problems, you come up with an equation, and then you solve for a number that gives you the answer. In life, though, your intuition is all you have.

You don't know, but you know.

Men are just like boys, only older.

"I'm sorry, Faithy," he says. "This just isn't cool," he says.

He's smoked my cigarette down to nothing. I reach into my purse, fumbling for my pack, and take out another one. I feel my knife nestled down at the bottom, and I take it out, too, click it open. He doesn't even see it because he's staring out at his stupid yard, pretending I'm already gone. I'm not there in the above-ground plastic pool they used to have, or eating a grilled hot dog or marshmallow from the end of a stick. I'm not with Heather in her room, or sitting next to her at the dinner table, taking the basket of rolls from her hand, passing them to Mrs. Phillips.

"So..." Barry says.

"So, what?" I say.

"I'd better be getting back to bed."

He flicks the dead cigarette butt off the porch into the bushes. "I'm sorry," he says. "If Leslie catches me, I'm dead."

I sit there, turned away from him on the swing, holding the knife in my lap. I could turn, before he gets up, and stab him in the heart, and then he really would be dead. I could get away with it. I could say, *He touched me between my legs. He forced me. He took me to the Tip Top Motel, and said he would hurt me if I ever told.* Everyone knows what men do to girls; people would believe it was self-defense. No one would know the truth.

I put a fresh cigarette in my mouth. I close the knife and drop it back into my purse. I take out my Bic, and in the light of the little butane flame, I see Barry's face. It's the face of a scared boy, afraid of what he wants, afraid of what I might need from him, and he doesn't even know how dangerous I am. I bring the tip of my cigarette to the light and take a deep drag. I sit smoking, while he doesn't move. I stare out into the tiny, familiar yard, taking my time, and when I finish the cigarette, I put it out on the arm of the swing and drop the butt into my purse.

"Barry," I say. It's all I can manage, and it sounds wrong.

I stand up. He's got his head lowered. He's staring at his hands, or something. I think about walking home in my night-gown, the moonlight all over me like I'm nothing but a ghost. But what I do is this. I go back inside the Phillipses' house, up the stairs, into Heather's room. I open the door quietly, and it closes again with the slightest click. Heather is lying on her back, the blankets bunched around her. I get into bed beside my friend, and pull the covers over us.

ANOTHER BREAKUP SONG

They broke up with *Fuck you*. They broke up with her standing in front of the door trying to block it to keep him from leaving—he was big, nearly twice her size—and repeatedly patting her head. Patting was the "timeout" gesture they had agreed on after reading a chapter of a self-help book about anger. She had bought the book after a particularly nasty argument, and when she had asked him to read it with her they'd gottten into another argument; he did not believe a book could solve anything, whereas a book was the first thing she thought of, and she was angry because, as she finally told him, he did not really want to solve their problems if he would not even read a book, which was all that she was asking him to do, and then they spent an evening in bed reading a chapter aloud and outlining on a worksheet exactly what had happened during their last nasty argument. They agreed that their arguments had escalated, usually did escalate, in a bad way, and that they needed a signal for the next time things began to spiral.

Filling out the worksheet had made her feel like they were getting somewhere. Step by step, they went over what had happened, and agreed on exactly the moment things had started to go south. All they needed was to stop the process before that point. When they finished, he put the book on the table on his side of the bed, and they talked seriously, while he held her. Then, with considerable laughter, they suggested to each other what signal might be the one that either of them could use to alert the other that they had gone too far and were starting to lose control. Making a "T" with their hands, for "Timeout," seemed too predictable. She tugged on her ear; he went cross-eyed and stuck out his tongue; she did her bat imitation, baring her teeth and smashing her nose with her index finger so the nostrils flared. He made his sad sack face and adopted his funny Italian accent, and she answered with baby talk. The head pat seemed to strike the right note—during an argument, it would be somewhat comic, but not disrespectful. It would lighten things up just enough to avert catastrophe.

But the catastrophe had already started, and there was no way to stop it. It would have been like trying to stop a tsunami after the tectonic plates ground against each other and the earth shifted on its axis. They broke up with her drunkenly, wildly, patting her head like some intoxicated chimp that had been taught to sign. Later, when she could try to find it funny, she imagined a group of animal scientists, plying the chimp with gin to see whether it would still remember to communicate as the humans had taught it.

But really, it wasn't at all funny at the time. He left, with her saying, *Stay, just stay and argue and fight with me or whatever, but please don't leave me.* He practically ran out, having gathered up his leather jacket and the blue backpack he usually brought when he spent the night.

A few minutes after he left, she noticed his belt on an armchair. She went outside and saw his car, still parked across the street. He was sitting in it, either getting ready to go or trying to cool down. Possibly he was even thinking about coming back to her apartment, which is what he'd done the last time, after the nasty argument that had led to reading the book about anger. But when he saw her, he started his car and pulled away from the curb. She ran into the street and threw his belt at the taillights and then he was gone and the belt lay there in the street like a dead snake.

Back inside she felt terrible about everything as usual, and as usual, she started calling him. She forgot whatever she said on the phone, to his voicemail. The only message she remembers is the one that said, *You're wrong for me anyway,* in a slightly bitter voice, the kind of voice she got when she was drunk and unhappy, the voice she knew he hated, that was sure to drive him even further away.

Then she started texting him. They were sarcastic texts, because she felt hurt and wanted to hurt him, too, though really she loved him and never wanted to hurt him, ever, and felt ashamed that she couldn't stop herself. The final text said, *If this is how you're going to treat me then we're done, I really mean it,* and after a couple of hours, when he didn't answer any of the texts or phone calls and she felt sober enough to drive, she went outside and picked up his belt from the middle of the street and drove to his house.

One of his roommates opened the door. She went upstairs to his bedroom. It was dark in there, and he was in bed, under the covers. She walked over to the bed. The room smelled like him. His banjo was hung on one wall, its strings glinting a little in the light coming in from the hallway. She could hear his roommates downstairs, laughing while they played a video game, their video assault rifles going off.

She said, *Here's your belt*, and he didn't move. He lay there, curled up like a giant sad baby. She couldn't even hear him breathe. She turned and laid the belt, coiled into a neat zero, on his desk under the window, and then she left, and she never saw him again. All this was a couple of years ago. He was her first real love after college. She was reckless, and drank too much, and nothing ever worked out. But maybe if she'd moved closer to the bed then and said, *Baby, I'm so sorry, please forgive me, I love you,* or whatever else she felt in that moment, in just the right tone of voice, it would have been different, but she didn't, and couldn't, and now she has this.

CANCER POEMS

When Ruth walks into the community college classroom for the second meeting of Introduction to Poetry, she looks around and realizes that only the crazies are left. On the teacher's desk is a pile of drop slips from the normal people who had introduced themselves last week. "Hi, I'm Cindy and I'm applying to Mills College." "My name is John. I wanted to, like, try to write some poems and I'm way into Bukowski, he's awesome." Normal Berkeley kids, with steel balls in their pierced tongues and thin silver rings sticking out of their eyebrows. But those students are gone, Ruth sees, as she takes a seat in the second-to-last row. They have better ways to spend a Thursday night: concerts, movie-and-pizza dates, petting in their parents' basements drunk on stolen liquor. They are young and healthy and optimistic. She would not be here if she were any of those things. The desk she eases into has a flip-up writing surface she has to struggle to lift from its collapsed position and screaks loudly as she wrestles with it. The other students look at her, but no one offers to help.

Next to Ruth is a man who probably, like her, has seen the other side of sixty. At the first class, he had said, "I see words on people's foreheads, and I just write them down." Tonight, as last week, he is in a camouflage outfit, the visor of his cap pulled low—possibly to keep others from reading whatever is written on his own forehead. In the front row is the bipolar man who announced, smirking, "I have three children and an unfortunate history of madness," and next to him is a woman with long gray braids and filthy Birkenstocked feet, who sits with crossed arms, staring balefully around the room. Behind her slouches the girl raped by her uncle, and behind *her* is the one who tried to kill herself twice. Already, Ruth knows far more about these people than she wants to. Last week, when it was her turn to say something, she just told them her name and her former occupation, technical editor. She wasn't about to say cancer or brain tumor, nausea or chemo or MRI. She wasn't going to say, stage four.

Ruth's desktop has crashed to the side and must be lifted once more. Now the other students are completely ignoring her. "Fuckwads," Camouflage Man says in Ruth's direction, possibly as a gesture of solidarity.

For this, Ruth had quit Cancer Support: seven fellow doomed souls and a Jesuit priest, a gentle man who spooked easily. A clap of thunder outside, a car backfiring, a heavy book falling to the floor—each time Father Andrew had cringed like an abused dog. Cancer Support was no help to Ruth. In an ugly room at Kaiser Permanente they drank decaf with Mocha Mix and traded recipes for pot brownies and cookies, and no one dared to get vehement, for fear of upsetting Father Andrew. "Visualize your body filling with blue light," Father Andrew said, but Ruth's body was filled with insects—hideous cockroaches swarming first her right lung and then her brain. Now they are waiting in the cracks of her body to finish her off. She has given up visualizing them scurrying away, or stomped underfoot, or convulsing from Raid until they stiffen and lie still. Now she just hates them. She sees their tiny black eyes, the threads of their waving antennae, and hates.

The poetry teacher, Lily Yee, is late. Maybe she isn't coming. Maybe she, like the missing students, has more appealing things to do. Lily Yee has published two books of poems and gotten some grant or other. Surely she can do better than this gray-walled classroom with its scratched blackboards on three sides filled with hastily erased equations, x's and numbers still visible under the streaks of chalk. But here she comes, finally, brushing past Mark in his wheelchair by the door. Mark was hit by a car as he exited a taxi at the corner of Geary and Van Ness in San Francisco and is in the process of suing the lawyers who handled his case. When Lily Yee passes him, Mark whispers, "Hello, goddess," and she acts like she doesn't hear him.

"Hey, everybody," Lily Yee says, moving to stand behind the desk. She is a young Chinese American with a Louise Brooks haircut, a perky little thing in a beige skirt and jacket and pearl earrings. She does not fit Ruth's idea of a poetess. Ruth had expected extravagance of some kind—a wild mane of curls, turquoise and silver bracelets, a flowing, diaphanous dress. Lily Yee reminds Ruth of her downstairs neighbor, Amy Wong, an insurance agent for State Farm. Lily Yee smiles, showing brilliant teeth, blue-white and practically iridescent. Ruth wonders if she has gone to Brite Smile, like Amy.

"I see we got rid of the losers," Lily Yee says, indicating the drop slips with one brisk chop of her hand. "Good."

Ruth glances at Camouflage Man, next to her, who has started talking to the gray chest hairs sprouting from his open collar. "Goddamned shithams," he whispers, almost inaudibly. "Fartmongers. Scrubby groins."

Lily Yee calls the roll, and everyone responds a different way, as though they are already being asked for some creative, original language. The first student says, "Yo," the next one, "Yeah," the third waves his hand and says, "You betcha." "Present and accounted for," Mark calls from his wheelchair, and the suicidal girl, Heather, says, "Present?" with that annoying lilt so many young people have. "Present," Ruth calls out at her own name, and, perhaps because they have run out of interesting options, the rest of the students parrot her response.

Next, Lily Yee says she wants everyone to read aloud a poem they have written. She chooses a blond boy in faded black jeans and a black hooded sweatshirt, who last week introduced himself as Derek, with no added personal information.

"Pass, please," Derek says.

Lily Yee stops smiling. "Participation is required," she says slowly, enunciating it like she's speaking to someone who doesn't understand English. *Participation* is a word she used a lot last week. And *commitment*. That was probably the word that had scared off half the class.

Derek toys with a Starbucks cup on his desk. Ruth can't see his face. He's just a kid in a black hood, silent, his lanky legs and big Doc Marten boots thrust out.

"Okay, Derek," Lily Yee says finally, with what sounds like forced pleasantness. "We'll come back to you." Now her gaze falls on Ruth, and she gestures in her direction. "It's Ruth, isn't it?" she says, encouraging. "Why don't you start us off."

Ruth opens the journal she bought at Barnes & Noble. It's heavy, handmade, with pale yellow pages and a gold angel floating across its front cover. At the top of each page, an inspiring or instructive quotation by a writer is printed in italics. There's one Ruth likes, by Elmore Leonard: *I try to leave out the parts that people skip.* She reads that aloud to the class, and Lily Yee smiles her unnatural smile again. There is one poem in Ruth's journal so far, four lines about her daughter Eve's husband being a jerk at Shabbat dinner last week. "This is about my family," she says apologetically. She knows poetry is supposed to be about trees and stars and the ineffable beauty of the world; it is supposed to be sublime. But this is all she's got right now. She reads,

Arthur called Eve a goddamned bitch.
She should have had a good man, maybe rich.
He should have treated her like a queen.
Instead he acted like a fiend.

"I'm not sure if that last one is a proper rhyme," Ruth says. She looks down at her words, reliving the dinner: all she could manage to eat was the challah. Arthur had shoveled in scalloped chicken casserole with the fervor of a starving man. Rachel, Ruth's granddaughter, snuck a fistful of green beans into a napkin in her lap; Ruth saw, and winked at her. Eve drank a can of Slim Fast, instead of eating the meal she'd prepared. Poor Eve, overweight and miserable and married to Arthur the Shit. And all in front of Rachel, darling Rachel, apple of Ruth's eye, her cuppycake, her pumpy-umpy-umpkin.

After Arthur said "goddamned bitch" and left the table, the words hung in the air above his chair, refusing to dissolve.

"The bastard," a woman says suddenly. Ruth looks up. It's Elena, the woman of the gray braids and Birkenstocks.

"Thank you," Ruth says, not sure how to respond.

"Families," Elena says. "I could tell you some stories." She lets out a heavy sigh.

"Let's talk about Ruth's piece," Lily Yee says. "It's a good seed for a poem."

"A good seed," Ruth says. "But is it a good poem?"

Lily Yee stops smiling. When Ruth went to Pegasus Books in Berkeley and asked about poetry by Lily Yee, the clerk couldn't find anything in the computer and said she should try online, because Lily Yee's books were probably published by very small presses.

"How long have you been writing poetry?" Lily Yee asks, a tincture of frost in her voice.

"I wrote that yesterday," Ruth tells her. "It's my first one."

"Your first one. And you want to know if it's any good."

"A perfectly legitimate question," says a man named Rafael, who wears an eye patch. The patch is dark brown and matches the rest of his face, and from where Ruth sits he looks like he has blank skin where his eye is supposed to be. He speaks with a lisp, so it comes out sounding like "quethtion." "After all," he goes on, "why waithte your time on poetry if you have no thpecial talent for it?" Several people murmur their assent.

"Ah, talent," Lily Yee says. "What is talent?" She stands before them, wearing pale polish, a wedding ring, her hair stiff and shiny as plastic. She looks like Chinese Barbie. Ruth tries to imagine Lily Yee with her head shaved, dressed in a pale blue hospital gown, an IV itching in her arm. Ruth's hair has grown back, but it's wispy as duck-down where it used to be thick. Lily Yee taps her high-heeled sandal impatiently, waiting for someone to answer.

"Ability?" someone says, hesitant.

"Fathility," says the man with the eye patch.

"Exactly," Lily Yee says. "And how do you achieve ability, and facility, in poetry? Through *practice*," she answers herself. "You"—she turns her eyes to Ruth—"have not yet *practiced*. Of course it's not any good."

Ruth looks down at her journal. The lines on the pages are the turquoise of the Caribbean. There are colorful flowers writhing up the margins. She takes the page she wrote on, tears it out, and crumples it in her hand.

"I thought it was great," Heather, the suicidal girl, says. "I wouldn't change a word. I certainly wouldn't throw it away."

"Don't let other people tell you that you're no good," the girl in front of her says.

"Yeah, what does she know?" Now there is a chorus of voices, all affirming that Ruth has just presented a work of rare genius. But Ruth knows in her heart that Lily Yee is right; her poem is terrible.

Lily Yee has gone to stand near one of the blackboards, putting a long table between her and the students. She doesn't say anything, just stands there with her arms at her sides, looking at some papers scattered on the table. Finally she lifts her eyes and gazes at the far wall, over their heads, as though they have ceased to exist. She begins to intone words in a low voice, so that everyone has to lean forward to hear her.

"*My heart aches*," she says, "*and a drowsy numbness pains / My sense, as though of hemlock I had drunk, / Or emptied some dull opiate to the drains / One minute hence, and Lethewards had sunk.*"

There's dead silence in the room for several seconds.

"John Keats," Lily Yee says. "That takes *practice*."

There's more silence. Sid, the bipolar man, breaks it. "Depression," he says. "Been there, done that," Sid says.

• • •

Before her diagnosis, when she was working, Ruth had been miserable. She would lie awake nights, fantasizing scenarios that would rescue her from Bechtel forever. Winning the Super Lotto jackpot, or being romanced by a wealthy blind man who wouldn't know that her hair was gray, her arms wrinkling, her eyelids drooping. Every weekday, as she stood in the Casual Carpool line waiting for a ride across the Bay Bridge into San Francisco, she was slammed with dread at the thought of her ergonomically correct workstation, the tedious manuals that crossed her desk, the bovine engineers, pale and constantly chewing Nicoret, who came looking for them. But now that she's on permanent disability, she's bored out of her skull, and she misses her old routines. All she has now is chemo. She was supposed to have been dead six months ago. She's supposed to be grateful for the extra time, to see each day as a blessing. What a crock.

It was Eve who had browbeaten her into taking a poetry class. Eve had plucked a shocking pink flyer from the library's bulletin board and presented it to her mother. Eve cried, which always worked. "You can't just rot in your apartment," Eve had said, when she found out Ruth quit Cancer Support.

"Rot," Ruth had said. "Nice choice of words. Soon enough, I'll rot. Right now I'm just shitting my brains out."

"Mom, Mom, Mom," Eve said, through her tears.

"I'll be all right, *kinehora*." An expression her mother had used, to ward off the evil eye. "Why would I be interested in poetry?"

"You could write a few things down. For me and Rachel. Especially for Rachel, to remember you."

"What, not remember me? How could she forget her *bubbe*, that scrawny, sickly woman in the head scarf?"

Ruth's own mother had been sickly for many years, but glamorously so. She had spent her days in a red Japanese silk robe, white cranes flying up toward one elegant shoulder. She had played Chopin on a gleaming baby grand, and lain on the couch in the apartment in Brooklyn like a fading movie star while her husband and friends attended her, while more friends came by with whole chickens and cakes and kugel. She had not died alone; when she finally passed, the same year Rachel was born, the room had been so crowded it was hard to breathe.

Maybe, Ruth thought later, her mother had succumbed in the end to simple oxygen deprivation, all those loved ones taking up the air.

"Mom, please," Eve said. "I got you a laptop. You can sign up online."

Alone in bed in her Oakland apartment, Ruth listens to her whirring fan and imagines it's a quiet outboard motor. She is lying in a boat, headed out toward the middle of a wide lake. The water is perfectly flat and still and black, the pupil of a flattened eye. The third class is tomorrow. Ruth has read the poems in the anthology Lily Yee asked everyone to buy, but she hasn't done the writing assignment. Lily Yee has told them about specifics, about details, about writing from the body. Ruth had to laugh at that one, in class, and Lily Yee flashed her a quick look. But, fine, she'll write from the rotting, roach-infested body. It's after midnight, and she feels exhausted, but she can't sleep. Might as well put something down on paper.

She sits at her kitchen table with her journal, after making some of the foul-tasting herb tea the acupuncturist prescribed. Her cat, Miss Thing, tries to leap onto her lap, and Ruth shoves her off. After whining for a while, Miss Thing settles her heavy body over Ruth's feet. Ruth sits there paralyzed, staring at the sappy expression on the angel's face, wondering what she has to write about. She thinks of what Lily Yee said: *Of course it's not any good.* My poetry is bad, Ruth thinks. It's like the parts that people skip. I don't have time to *practice.*

Finally she opens the journal at random, to a quote by someone named Lawrence Clark Powell. *Writing is a solitary occupation. Family, friends, and society are the natural enemies of a writer. He must be alone, uninterrupted, and slightly savage if he is to sustain and complete an undertaking.*

Ruth stands up, dislodging the cat. She feels like the words have flown off the page and are frantically circling the kitchen, banging their wings against the window, the yellow walls, the hanging pots and pans. She goes back to the journal and reads them again. Solitary. Alone. She must be uninterrupted, she must be savage. Ruth sees herself forging through dense jungle growth, enormous vines whipping her face. Fat snakes dangle from the trees. In the darkness, predatory animals are crouching, waiting to spring, their red eyes laser points of light.

Ruth decides she is going to do more than put down a few thoughts for Eve and Rachel. She is going to write an entire book, a book Rachel will read one day. She'll have to hurry, though. Keats didn't have much time, either, she had discovered. He had died young, feverish and coughing up blood. It wasn't a stretch to imagine it.

She first writes a poem called "Lust," about her ex-husband. She was in the kitchen of their house in St. Thomas, making chicken with raspberry sauce while Frank showered. The bathroom door was open, and from the shower he looked down the hall and saw her leaning her elbows on the counter, her sexy ass thrust out, as he later put it. He came into the kitchen dripping wet, opened the freezer and took out one of the frozen bananas Ruth liked to dip in chocolate and nibble on in the evenings, then led her to the bedroom. She writes about what happened in the bedroom. Next she writes about Robert, a man in Cancer Support who died and was buried in a black silk dress as he requested, and then about showing Rachel how to eat a pomegranate. She fills page after page of her notebook, scrawling furiously, crossing out, drawing arrows to the next lines, hardly knowing what she's doing.

By the time she stops writing, gray light eases in through the blinds. The tea sits beside her, cold and untouched. She feels like she did when she woke up from the surgery, when she opened her eyes on the gurney in the recovery room and didn't know who or even what she was, as though the doctors had actually removed her brain and not just a tumor. She moves toward her bedroom slowly, the room going in and out of focus. She crawls into bed and covers herself with all the blankets.

A bird starts up outside. Miss Thing races over to jump onto the bed, and then onto the shelf under the window. She sits looking out, making the low sound in her throat that means she's hunting. Ruth thinks of the Keats poem that Lily Yee had recited—"Ode to a Nightingale." Afterwards she had handed out a copy to everyone. Ruth feels for the lamp on the nightstand, searching for the button on its base, knocking the TV remote and a couple of pill bottles to the floor. She finds the switch, takes the folded copy of the poem from the nightstand, and reads aloud.

Thou wast not born for death, immortal bird. It comes out weak and raspy. In Lily Yee's resonant voice the poem was like amber rum, a smooth, intoxicating pour of words. In Ruth's, it sounds like lemonade without enough sugar. But she goes on, anyway. *No hungry generations tread thee down.* And soon comes her favorite part of the poem, the part about the song *that found a path / Through the sad heart of Ruth,* poor homesick Ruth, *in tears amid the alien corn.* She finishes reading that stanza and lies back, sweating, pushing away the blankets. It's worse than menopause, worse than the hot flashes and the hormones careening through her bloodstream. It will pass in a few minutes. Or else, as sometimes happens, it won't, and while the cramps slice through her she will curl up in her bed or on the bathroom floor so she can stay close to the toilet.

She reaches over the edge of the bed for the pills that fell. She wonders how much time it will take, how many poems she'll need to make a book.

• • •

"Anyone want to start?" Lily Yee says. She has had the students arrange their desks in a circle, and has explained the rules for the workshop, or critique session. The writer is to read his or her poem aloud, and then they all tell the writer what they think of it. During this time, the writer is not allowed to speak.

Ruth has decided to present the poem about Rachel and the pomegranate, because she doesn't want to tell these people about being made love to with a frozen banana, or about Cancer Support. She typed it on her new laptop and made thirteen copies at Kinko's, for the twelve students and for Lily, who presides over them from the table at the side of the room.

Elena, of the gray braids and dirty feet, Elena of the shapeless tie-dyed dress and a large bead necklace that looks heavy as rocks, wants to begin. "I only want positive feedback," she says.

Everyone looks at Lily Yee to see if this is allowed.

"We are going to be honest," Lily Yee says. "Honest feed-back is a gift for any writer."

"I can't handle criticism," Elena says.

"We'll be gentle," Lily Yee says.

Ruth can hear steel in Lily Yee's voice. She's not going to let Elena off. Good.

Elena passes around copies of her poem, which is called "My Pain." Each line begins, "My pain is..." and then characterizes it. Elena's pain is a drum, a dog, a sinking ship. But at the end, her pain turns golden, and burns. *Like the sun*, she has written. *Like the glorious, glorious, sun.* Elena's voice rises, expands, as though it is the burning sun itself, washing everyone in rays of glory. Even Ruth realizes how bad Elena's poem is.

When Elena finishes, no one says anything. She looks around the circle of desks and then slumps in hers.

"There's a lot of emotion here," Lily Yee says finally. "And," she says, "look at all the metaphors! We haven't gotten to met-aphors yet, but, ah, wow. Look, here they are."

Ruth is disappointed in Lily Yee. She expected her to say something else. That Elena's poem lacks specifics. That it's not from the body. That Elena has no right to go on as though her pain is so almighty important, when Elena likely still has thirty-odd more years to shuffle around in tie-dyed sacks.

"It sucks," Mark says flatly, shifting in his wheelchair.

"Respectful feedback," Lily Yee admonishes him. "You don't think this is a successful piece, Mark? Can you tell Elena why?"

"It's boring," Mark says.

"Well, I wasn't bored," Suicidal Heather says. "I really liked the part about the pain cutting like a knife."

"Yes," Lily Yee says. "And that's a simile, a comparison using like or as. Now, the next step, Elena, would be to make it a fresher, more unique comparison."

"It says exactly what I want it to say," Elena tells her.

"All right then," Lily Yee says, and there's that edge in her voice again. "Then we'll just move on. Mark, since you were the first to comment on Elena's poem, why don't we look at yours next."

Mark's poem is incomprehensible, a bunch of words strung together that nobody understands. When a few people tell him this, he leans back in his chair with a superior smile. Lily Yee tries to ask him what he was trying to say, but he won't tell anyone. They go around the circle like this, reading, arguing, asking questions. Bipolar Sid reads about fondling himself in a mental institution: he does it downy, he does it uppy, he cuffs his puppy. Lily Yee points out the use of metaphor again. She explains slant rhyme and suggests that it might be more successful than the direct rhymes of "uppy" and "puppy," "jack off" and "whack off," but nobody agrees with her.

Ruth is sitting next to the table, on Lily Yee's left, and is the last to read. She's so nervous she can barely get out the words. When she finishes there's the usual harrowing silence, and the first thing anyone says is, *Is Rachel black?*

"No," Ruth says. "Her father, Arthur, is Filipino."

"You wrote, 'her brown skin,'" Elena says. "When I think of brown skin, I think of a black person."

"Well, I don't," Rafael with the eye patch says. "*I'm* not a black perthon."

Keturah, the young girl abused by her uncle, who *is* black, says, "Please say African American."

Ruth looks down at her poem while they continue their discussion. She doesn't know if what she's written is any good, and she is afraid to ask. *I'm not a writer*, she thinks. *I don't have the time to become one. This class is not going to help.*

"This part?" It's Derek, the boy who wouldn't participate last week. The hood of his sweatshirt is pushed back off his face, and to Ruth he looks about twelve. "Where you talk about how Rachel chews the seeds?" he says. "This part is cool. And the stuff about your mother, too, how she showed you the way to eat them. So it's like passing something on to the next generation."

"Thank you," Ruth says.

"Yes," Lily Yee chimes in. "But remember not to assume that this is Ruth's life. Remember, we refer to the speaker, or the narrator, of the poem. So it's the speaker's cousin who says, '*Ze bist ein shiksa,*' thinking that the little girl is a non-Jew. And the speaker replies, 'No, this is *mein tuchter's kindelah.* My daughter's child.' That is," Lily Yee says, "the speaker's daughter's child."

"But Ruth's the speaker," Derek says. "And Rachel is your granddaughter, right?" he says, turning to Ruth.

"Do you have any pictures of her?" Elena says.

"It's a convention," Lily Yee says, "and we're going to follow it in this class."

"Yeah," Derek says. "Whatever."

. . .

Before Introduction to Poetry, Ruth's knowledge of the art consisted of a few vague memories: the tree pressing itself to the earth's sweet swelling (or was it smelling?) breast, the noble six hundred riding into the mouth of Hell, Hiawatha waiting by the shore of Gitchie-Gumee. She had read technical journals for work. She read novels, and cookbooks, and an occasional popular memoir. Now she has no use for anything but poetry. It's like great gulps of air. She feels she is beginning to understand the beauty of the sentence and the line, the spark of metaphor. She doesn't really get meter yet, but Lily Yee promises they are going to study it more.

Every week now Ruth types up several poems on her laptop, then chooses one for class. So far she has brought the poem about feeding the ducks at Lake Merritt with Rachel, and one about mountain biking with Frank and falling face-first in a cowpat. She titled it "Eating Shit." The class laughed, though Lily Yee looked pained. Last week she brought the one about the frozen banana. Mark, who usually acted like he couldn't care less, wheeled over to Ruth at the break and said she must have been one hot mama. Ruth was pleased, because she knew Mark already had a crush on Lily Yee and on Derek as well, and neither one of them would give him the time of day, and Mark was miserable over them. For him to stir himself enough to compliment her was a good sign.

But this week, all she has written are cancer poems. One after another they churn from the printer at Kinko's, poems to a God she doesn't believe in, descriptions of chemo treatments and mad, broken cells run amok. When Ruth writes from the body, what comes out is humiliation and disease. In class, when her turn to read comes, she passes. She bows her head at Lily Yee's disapproving look.

All the next week, though she tries to write about other things, it's the same: cancer poems. She skips class that Thursday. She sits in her bed, thinking about the other students, wondering if anyone misses her. Maybe she won't go back. When she quit Cancer Support, a couple of people had called, but then they stopped. Life goes on, even in Cancer Support; the ties that bind, Ruth thinks, don't bind very hard, or for very long. She grabs a pen and writes in her journal, *ties that bind.* "Cliché," she can hear Mark saying. Lily Yee: "Aim for the newly imagined, not the already imagined." She crosses out the words.

The following week she forces herself to go to class. The poem she reads doesn't actually have the word cancer in it, but it's pretty clear. At least, she thinks it is, until the discussion starts.

"Ruth, honey," Phyllis says. "What's it all about, Alfie?" Phyllis started the class as Phil, but then he showed up wearing purple fingernail polish and read a poem called "The Girl in the Mirror," and confessed he was a pre-op tranny, which is what transgender people apparently call themselves. "And *I vote*," he said, looking at everyone defiantly. Ruth wondered how important the tranny vote might be to politicians. "Of course you vote, dear," Elena murmured, and ever since, he's been in tailored skirts and prim dresses, his long hair neatly clipped with a barrette. Everyone praised the emotional power of "The Girl in the Mirror." Ruth told Phyllis it was his best poem yet, that it made her understand what he was going through, and after class he blew Ruth a kiss.

"I don't get it," Phyllis says now. "What's so important to the speaker about seeing green fields and mud?"

"And the constellations on the speaker's arms," Camouflage Man says. "Stars on her arms?"

Words on their foreheads? Ruth wants to say.

"Is she cutting herself?" Heather asks. Heather's poems, every week, are about razors, pills, guns. She's a beautiful girl, beautiful and crazy. Ruth thinks Derek may like her— he loaned her money last week during the break, to get some of the awful-tasting coffee from the machine in the lounge. After class Ruth had suggested to Heather that she should pay Derek back with a better cup of coffee, some night before class. It would be a good thing for Heather, Ruth thinks, if they got together. Derek's quiet, but he's bright. He writes about growing up in Pittsburgh, about working to clean up industrial sites for the EPA, about Impressionist painting. Ruth bets he's never even considered the idea of leaving this world before he absolutely has to.

"Can I speak?" Ruth asks Lily Yee.

"Let's just see what people are getting from this," Lily Yee says, prolonging the torture.

"What's Rachmaninoff doing in the poem?" Phyllis says.

It's Bipolar Sid who actually gets it. "I think," he says, "the speaker is ill. She's talking about the things she loves. The stuff on her arms is bruises from some kind of medical procedure. She's driving to visit somebody—it's not clear who— but anyway, she's passing the fields of artichokes, those are the green fields. And the G-minor piano and cello sonata is on the radio, and then you're playing with your granddaughter in the mud somewhere; you really should explain that part, Ruth. And trying to feel, well, connected, to the things you want to take with you when you go."

Everybody looks at Sid. Sid's critical comments are usually restricted to two ironic words: *How lovely*. That's his stock response, whether it's Elena and her pain or one of Keturah's sappy love poems to her fiancé—she's engaged, and everybody refers to her now as The Bride. Ruth expects Sid to say, "Cancer. How lovely," any minute.

"The speaker," Lily Yee says.

The attention swings back to her. "The speaker is dying?" Lily Yee asks Ruth. "Is that what's happening here?"

"Bingo," Ruth says.

"Then you should clarify that point," Lily Yee says.

• • •

Lily Yee has given them an assignment to attend a poetry reading. It turns out you can go to one any night of the week in the Bay Area. Ruth goes with Derek, Heather, Elena, and Sid to an open mic in the basement of a brew pub. Sid is the only one of them who has enough courage to get up and read a poem.

"I call this one, 'Lament of the Lonely Fudgepacker,'" he says after clearing his throat at the mic. The room cracks up, and he reads to laughter and enthusiastic applause. Everyone drinks a lot of beer. Ruth mentions that she has pot at her apartment—it's the only thing that helps her keep any food down at all—and Derek and Heather insist on coming over to smoke some.

Ruth is embarrassed about her apartment, but Derek and Heather don't seem to notice the stacks of books and paper everywhere, the dust bunnies in the corners, dirty dishes from two days ago still on the kitchen counter. Heather sits on Ruth's couch, petting Miss Thing, and Derek settles onto the rug, cross-legged, and takes a small glass pipe from his backpack.

"Got any more to drink?" he calls to Ruth, who is in the kitchen hunting for any kind of snacks to offer them.

"I'll look." She used to enjoy the taste of wine. She finds a bottle in a bottom cupboard, an expensive cabernet she'd been saving. For what? Now is as good a time as any. She has nothing in the fridge but rye crackers. She arranges them on a plate and brings them out with the wine, glasses, and a corkscrew on a TV tray.

"I'll do it," Heather says. "I love opening wine."

Derek lights up, throws his head back as he holds in the smoke. After a minute he exhales. "Nice," he says, passing it up to Ruth, on the couch next to Heather.

"Thank you." Ruth is pleased that her medicinal marijuana from the Cannabis Buyers' Cooperative has passed muster.

Heather pours the wine, and they all clink glasses.

"I'll put on some music," Ruth says, wondering if she has anything they will like.

"Do you have that one you wrote about?" Heather says. "Romanoff?"

"Rachmaninoff," Derek says. "That's a beautiful sonata, the one in your poem."

"You know classical music?" Ruth says.

"My dad turned me on to it," Derek says. "He liked all those

Romantic guys. Brahms, Schumann, Tchaikovsky. Mahler especially."

Ruth goes to her CD rack and finds Mahler's Second, conducted by Leonard Bernstein. She takes her wine to the chair across from the couch, sits, and closes her eyes.

"Wow," Heather says after a while. "This is so cool. Too bad Sid and Elena couldn't come."

"Elena had to go home and feel her pain," Ruth says.

"And Sid—" Derek says. "Sid had to go home and cuff his puppy."

Ruth laughs so hard she farts, and then Heather nearly spits out her wine.

• • •

Lily Yee hosts a salon for the class in her living room, and they all read for each other and a few people's friends and spouses. The Bride brings her husband-to-be, a tall boy with a goofy smile who, to everyone's surprise, is white. Even Sid shows up with a girlfriend. Ruth has asked Eve, but Eve has Parent Night at Rachel's kindergarten, and Ruth wishes what she has often wished lately, to have someone beside her. Not Frank, though. Frank could hardly stand it when she had period cramps. He would have despised her now, if he could see how she sometimes struggles to get up from a deep chair or couch, how thin and weak she has become. And anyway Frank died five years ago. But someone besides Eve, who is busy with her own life. A man. Who might care for her enough to heat up some soup or bring her a damp washcloth. The loneliness feels worse than the cancer. *Writing is a solitary occupation.* She is alone. She must be a savage. A nauseous, trembling savage.

After the salon, she stays up late, reading over the poems she has written so far. She decides to change "brown skin" to "olive skin" in the poem about eating a pomegranate with Rachel. Lily Yee says revision is the most necessary part of writing. Revision will set you free, Lily Yee says. Ruth changes a couple more adjectives, eats two pot brownies, and goes to bed, floating above it, dreaming a tiger is stalking her through the halls of the college.

• • •

Just before Thanksgiving, the doctors find a new tumor. It is a hole in the x-ray, an almond-sized black spot on one ghostly white rib, and because of the location it is inoperable. They give her a few prescriptions. She hasn't been able to cry. She had cried when she was first diagnosed, and then almost every day during her first round of chemo—what everyone at Cancer Support had referred to as torture, as in, what are they torturing you with now? Now she sits. She sits on her couch, pushing away Miss Thing, and feels herself disappearing, getting small enough to slip through the black spot inside her.

Then it's Thanksgiving. Ruth sits on Eve and Arthur's couch with Arthur, watching a football game being played somewhere it is snowing, while Eve cooks. Rachel flits in and out in a long Victorian dress and a sparkly tiara and shimmery wings, hitting Ruth and then Arthur with a pinwheel she is using as a magic wand, until he yells at her and sends her to her room.

After dinner, Ruth lies down in the guest room, listening to Eve cleaning up in the kitchen, to the TV in the living room, to Rachel singing down the hall in her own room. It's some monotonous, repetitive song about a baby bumblebee. *Squishing the baby bumblebee...licking the baby bumblebee...throwing up the baby bumblebee...* In the morning, when she opens her eyes, Rachel is there—her solemn dark eyes, her olive skin.

"Want to go outside with me?" Rachel says.

Ruth eases herself down into an Adirondack chair in the front yard, wondering if she'll be able to stand up again. Rachel spins. Arms out, head thrown back, she turns circles until she staggers and then falls into the grass, breathing hard. Ruth starts to cry.

"What's the matter, *bubbe?*" Rachel says. "Are you sick again?" She comes over and climbs onto the arm of the chair.

The sun is bright, but not very hot. The sky is a washed-out, disappointing blue, and as Ruth sits there crying, she tries to think of a simile to describe what that blue is like.

Eve comes to the door and looks at them. "Mom, are you tired? Do you need to go home?"

"Home, roam, flown," Ruth says, trying to remember the differences between strict and slant rhyme, assonance and consonance. "Hymn. Rhyme. Flan. Moan. Alone. Gone. Bone."

"Ice cream cone," Rachel says.

. . .

When Eve was little, Ruth used to play a game with her. "I love you more," Ruth would say. "No," Eve would answer, "I love *you* more." Then Ruth would stretch out her arms and say, "I love you this much," and Eve would open hers and try to stretch them wider. Now Ruth plays the game with Rachel, in the bed in Eve and Arthur's guest room, when Rachel comes home from school. Miss Thing is with her, a furry lump at her feet. The house is quiet during the day and noisy in the evening. She sleeps on and off, a blanket over her head, listening to the TV, to nothing, waking to Rachel pulling the blanket down and looking into her eyes. Then Rachel disappears and Ruth falls into a well.

She puts one hand on the nightstand, bracing herself, and manages to sit up. An oval mirror hangs over the oak dresser against the far wall. Ruth goes over to it, shaking with the effort, one hand on the bed for support. The woman in the mirror is a hag. Her face is puffed-up and sallow. Small, angry red veins have burst on her cheeks and nose. She's a stranger, someone Ruth doesn't want to know. She wonders how anyone else can stand to look at her. She'd gotten up for a reason. What? What? She crawls back into bed.

She drifts on the morphine, back to St. Thomas. Sailing with Frank, wind smacking her hair off her face, sunlight flaring white on the galvanized tin roofs on shore. Her mother is playing a Chopin mazurka while Ruth sits under the piano, watching her mother's foot move on the pedals, her bare white foot that turns into a swan, rising and falling on a lake. Ruth is holding the infant Eve in her arms, gazing into her new daughter's eyes. But Eve is there, in the room.

"Ruth," Eve says, and dissolves into Penny, the home nurse.

"You smell like cigarettes," Ruth says.

"I'm quitting, I swear."

"I quit twenty-five years ago." But she means she quit loving Frank, who had left her. "I just stopped one day. I didn't even go to his funeral."

"Let's try to get a little food down, shall we?" Penny says.

One afternoon, Lily Yee calls. Eve brings in the phone, pats Ruth on the arm, and goes out.

"Ruth," Lily Yee says. "I'm so sorry to hear. Would you be up for a visit?"

"Why not," Ruth says. "How is everybody?"

"They all send their love."

Lily Yee brings the latest poems everyone has written. She sits in a chair beside the bed and reads a few aloud. Everyone has signed a Get Well card. *Miss you, Miss Ruth,* Phyllis has written. *We need more of your poems!* from The Bride. Rafael of the eye patch: *Write on.* Camouflage Man has drawn a heart with her name above it. *You are a queen among slatterns. Love from Mark. Don't let the bastards get you down. Luv, Elena.* Sid has written a line of Yeats, *How can we tell the dancer from the dance?* Derek has drawn a few bars of music—the opening of the Rachmaninoff sonata. But the best is from Heather, who writes, *Your poems make me want to live & drink wine haha.*

"I'm thirsty," Ruth says. She fumbles toward the nightstand for the water bottle. Lily Yee holds it so she can drink some through a straw. "Tell them—" Ruth says.

Lily Yee leans forward.

What? What? Ruth lies as still as possible, waiting for the pain to subside. "I was going to write a book," she tells Lily Yee. "A book of poems."

"Oh, big deal," Lily Yee says. "No one reads those slender little volumes of verse. They're good for tenure sometimes, though. Oh, I almost forgot." She reaches into her bag and brings out a pomegranate. "Derek thought of getting you this. Because of that poem you wrote, about showing Rachel how to eat it."

"Just put it here next to me." In the kitchen in Brooklyn, whitefish and sturgeon on the table. Her father still asleep. Her mother leans over a plate.

She shows me the red juice, the seeds.

"I think Derek and Heather are an item," Lily Yee says.

Her mother holds a seed between her teeth.

"He brought her a sunflower last class and laid it across her desk. You should have seen her blush."

Mein tuchter's kindelah. My daughter's child.

"Do you want me to read to you some more?"

Now I will show her what you showed me.
We take, we eat. We go down
into the earth, and are mourned.

"Ruth," Lily Yee says.

Fled is that music.

"Yes," Ruth says.

Miss Thing leaps from the end of the bed onto the oak dresser and looks out the window, drawn by the sound of some loud, screechy bird. A jay, Ruth thinks. The sky. But not that blue. A different blue. What, what?

"You have your cat with you," Lily Yee says.

"Yes."

"That's good."

Immortal bird.

"Yes."

Remember me.

ICE

Last night I dreamed I killed my brother. With an ax. I chopped off his right hand at the wrist, and he bled forever. Then I went home and forgot about him, until my mother called to tell me he was gone. And this was the *good* brother. I don't know why I had to dream about killing him, when it's the other one I wish were dead, dead, dead, dead, dead.

I'm going around my mother's rink on the Zamboni machine, thinking about my dream, trying to smooth it into the ice. I took a Valium but it's starting to wear off, and I want to get the ice done so I can take another. The sound of the blade shaving the surface of the ice, the shavings being propelled into the snow tank, the water being vacuumed up, all those sounds are setting my teeth on edge.

It's a Wednesday afternoon in December, and Lunch Skate is finished. Next there's a group lesson, followed by Senior Skate. Senior Skate used to be fifty-five and over, but when my mother hit fifty-five last year she raised it to sixty. I look over at the big glass window of the office, and she's there, at the computer, a mug of coffee beside her. The rink is open until ten every night and she's there then, too. When I'm home I wait up for her, to make sure she hasn't been attacked by a mugger while closing up. She says I shouldn't wait. She says I should get my own place, that at twenty-four I'm too old to live with her, but I know she doesn't mean it, because then she makes us both some Swiss Miss hot chocolate and settles on the couch with me to watch the talk shows.

My jerk of a brother is in the pro shop right now, hunched over an X-Men comic instead of taking inventory. I can see him after I complete the turn at the far end. He looks up, and I know I'm in trouble unless my good brother hurries up and gets here to teach the group lesson. What my jerk of a brother likes to do is accuse me of something like hiding a shipment of costumes, or the scheduling book, then grab my arm and pinch it until a bruise forms, or twist my arm behind my back and shove me against the wall so my head bangs against it. He does it with our mother in the next room, and he knows I won't cry out, or say anything later. It would kill her to find out how things still are, when she thinks all that stopped a long time ago.

When I pass the window of the office again my mother looks up and waves. I crank the Zamboni to top speed, about nine miles an hour, and wave back, my hand moving like a wiper blade, smoothing the air between us.

. . .

I finish my last sweep of the ice and park the Zamboni. To get to my mother in the office I have to go through the pro shop, and my bad brother is still there, waiting for me. Lately he's been hearing voices. I don't know what they say to him, but it isn't anything cheerful. He let his beard grow all over his face, and his hair has gotten long and curly, and he's pretty much stopped showering. He skulks around reeking of beer and pot, his head cocked, right ear aimed at the ceiling. I stop at the soda machine, stalling for time, then go into the bathroom and wash down a Valium with a Diet Coke. I sit on a toilet lid for a while, and when the Valium comes on I slowly head out, floating past the pay lockers, looking to see if a customer's in the pro shop so I can slip safely by.

There's my good brother, coming in from the parking lot through the double doors, bringing sunlight and joy and protection. We reach the door of the pro shop at the same time, and he lets me go in first. My other brother glances up at me, his gray eyes moving behind his glasses like a couple of sharks.

"Hi," I say and head for the door of the office. *I wish you were dead*, I think at him, as loud as I dare to. My brother has come close to death, but not nearly close enough. When we were younger he tried to kill himself with sleeping pills and vodka in the laundry room of our parents' house. He woke up on the floor, looking at all the lint that had gathered between the dryer and the wall. He told me about it once, during a brief period when he'd decided to be my friend. I listened and nodded. I didn't say anything about what happened right afterwards, when he came upstairs to find me and slam the back of my head with the vodka bottle.

I walk up behind my mother's chair and kiss the part in her graying hair. "All done," I say. "The ice is ready." Ready to be ruined, ready to be marked and scratched instead of pristine and wet and shiny. "I guess I'm done for the day."

"Can you stay?" she says. "Your brother has an appointment."

I can imagine my brother's appointment. He has an appointment with a DVD he wants to watch, or an ounce of pot he just scored, or some CDs he wants to buy with the money she gives him. He's supposed to work four days, but he doesn't show up half the time, or else he leaves early. Without her, he'd probably be homeless. When he moved out of her townhouse, she bought him a condo to live in. Last year, when he fell asleep with a cigarette and burned down his place and two others, she paid for all that and bought him another condo.

"He has to go meet a friend," my mother says. "I'm sure he'll do better, having a buddy to spend time with."

"Yeah," I say, rubbing her shoulders, worrying she's getting too thin.

"I think he'd perk up if he could find a girlfriend. He needs to meet a nice girl."

"Absolutely," I say, thinking, fat chance.

My brother doesn't have any friends. As for girlfriends, women won't give him the time of day. He walks up to them in bars when they're with their boyfriends or husbands, and hands them business cards he had made that say he's a poet, printed with his name and phone number and a few lines of his crappy verse, and of course they never call.

"I can stay." I kiss the top of her head again, inhaling the smell of her Herbal Essences shampoo. "I love you, Mom."

"Of course, honey," she says, but she's looking at something on the computer, and I know my words have slid right over her, as usual; the only one she thinks about is him.

. . .

My mother was a famous figure skater, a World and Olympic competitor. In the office she has all her trophies, and pictures of her younger self in skimpy sequined costumes, caught in a scratch spin or double axel. She taught for years, but my good brother gives most of the lessons now, my brother who is beloved by everyone; he is over six feet tall, and his brown eyes are the kind of liquid, compassionate eyes possessed by German Shepherds, and when you are around him you feel slightly more alive than you did in the moments before you entered his presence. I've seen him have this effect on complete strangers. It's probably due to him, as much as to my mother's reputation, that skating has become so popular in our Southern California town.

Right now, the ice is crowded with his students, little kids who zoom around and grab the edge of his zippered sweatshirt while he turns circles, laughing. I'm leaning my elbows on the counter of the pro shop, breathing freely since my asshole brother left.

The kids are working on crossovers now. *Trust the edge,* I can imagine my brother saying. *The edge will hold you up.* I've watched him give a million lessons.

Mrs. Saunders comes in, late, with her little girl. I thump down a pair of white figure skates, size 3. She looks at the other mothers sitting in the stands, then out to the ice.

"Your brother's such a darling," she says. She knows I have two, but we both know which one she means.

"He's a prince," I say.

"Does he have a girlfriend?" She asks it in a kind of casual way that I instantly sense is fake. I just look at her. "My husband and I are separated," she says. Like I accused her of adultery or something.

"That's too bad," I say politely.

"Not really. He was fucking the babysitter. The *male* babysitter," she adds. "I'm getting everything. The kid, the house, the condo on Catalina." She laughs, and I feel sorry for her. "How's your other brother?"

"You mean the problem child?"

"Who's a problem child?" my mother says, coming in from the office.

My bad brother was the truly talented one, at least that's what my mother thinks. She coached him relentlessly when he was little. She had him up at six a.m. every day before school, practicing. As a junior he was a rising star. He made it through the regionals and into the sectionals, but he came in fifth, and only the top four get to go on to the U.S. Nationals. Plus, in almost every competition he'd get in a fistfight with somebody, and pretty soon no one would let him on the ice.

"Oh, kids," Mrs. Saunders says. "They're all problem children. I'd better help Dakota." She goes over to a nearby bench her daughter is standing unsteadily in front of, wearing the unlaced skates.

"I don't appreciate that attitude," my mother says.

"What attitude?"

"Making fun of him."

"I wasn't." I stay at the window, not turning around.

"He tries," she says. "He really does."

"Not nearly hard enough," I can't help saying.

"Are you going to take inventory? Or just stand there all day staring into space?" She doesn't wait for me to answer. She goes back into the office and closes the door.

In the dream last night, when my mother called to tell me my good brother was dead, she didn't even sound sad. I watch him on the ice, taking Dakota by the hand and coaxing her forward—her ankles are wobbling like crazy—and I feel really terrible about that dream.

I had this therapist once who said that everyone in your dreams is really you. I didn't like her after that, because if she was right, it meant that after my father died, at the end of my senior year of high school, he hadn't really visited me in my dreams. In one dream I had just after his death, my brothers and I were wrapping him in a sheet to bury him in the backyard of the house we all lived in then. The yard was full of rocks and trophies. He was completely wrapped up, except for his face, and he smiled at me as we were carrying him, a peaceful, beatific smile. That dream made me feel a whole lot better about my father's death, until this therapist came along. According to her, I was trying to bury some part of myself. When she started having me hit a futon with a plastic baseball bat, pretending it was my bad brother, I gave up on her.

. . .

During Senior Skate, I take everyone's six dollars and ask them what size skates they want, even though I know their sizes by heart. It's the same people every week. Every Saturday there's a birthday party, with balloons and cake and little kids racing around and falling down on the ice and crying, and every Friday and Saturday night the kids from the junior high show up and the music changes to hip-hop or techno or whatever they're into. Every summer my good brother runs the Youth Hockey Camp, and Friday and Sunday mornings the pickup adult hockey games go on. We've got Public Sessions, the Coffee Club, Mom and Tot Classes, Individual and Group Lessons. We've got Free Skate Rental on Thursday nights, and we're open every single day of the year including Christmas, which my mother would probably work straight through if she could get away with it.

I've already told her that this year she's got to close or find somebody to cover the office, and that we've got to have a real tree. Up until two years ago we had a metal one, with silver branches you stuck into holes on the metal trunk, that we hung with the same blue ornaments, fragile balls that broke one by one and never got replaced. Finally even my mother noticed how the branches had gotten flattened and twisted over the years, and she threw it out. Last year, she stayed at the rink until eight-thirty Christmas night and then sent me to the gourmet grocery for a pre-made dinner. She hung the last of the blue bulbs on a potted plastic ficus, handed us all checks, and then we sat down to dinner until she had to go back and close the rink. My good brother gave her one of the miniature pianos she collects, and I gave her White Rose perfume. My bad brother gave her one of his homemade rap CDs filled with his deep insights into life, that he thinks are going to put him up there with Eminem and 50 Cent. Nobody mentioned the fact that she doesn't have a CD player, since my brother has a shorter fuse than usual when he's drinking.

In the last half hour of Senior Skate, Mrs. Harding shows up. She's wearing a lime-green pants suit, carrying her skates in a black canvas bag. She sets a roll of quarters on the counter.

"Mrs. Harding," I say. "Nice to see you again."

Mrs. Harding was out of action for a while with a hip replacement. I'm impressed that she's getting back on the ice.

"So," Mrs. Harding says. "You dating anyone yet? Got a beau?"

"No. You?"

It's what we always say. She's supposed to say, At my age, who needs them, like always. But instead she smiles, and winks. "Maybe," she says.

"Really." I dig my thumbnail into the wood of the counter. It's a bad habit, a thing I do when I'm nervous or upset. There are little gouges all over the counter, that look like they've all been made by setting skates, blade-down, in front of customers. I can't tell which are mine.

"You should find someone. Never too late," she says, as if I'm an old lady like her, as if I spend my nights alone and half my days in a bright red skirt that's way too short for me. "Live a little," she says.

"I do."

Mrs. Harding goes to change and lace up. She comes out and steps onto the ice, turns, and takes off backwards.

.   .   .

231

I don't have any problem finding someone. I go to a bar or a club, I dance with a boy or let him buy me a few drinks, and after closing, we go to his place. When we're done I leave right away, writing down a fake phone number if he asks for one. Sometimes I'll say, *Call me anytime. If I don't pick up, be sure to leave your number on my voicemail. I always return people's phone calls*, I say.

The bar closest to home is called the Knock-Knock Club. I like it because it's dark inside day or night, and because it's walking distance. It's also very festive during holidays. To-night there are blue lights strung behind the bar. "MERRY CHRISTMAS," in gold letters, hangs across the middle of the room. A six-foot Douglas fir is set between the doors to the bathrooms, dripping with tinsel and homemade ornaments—the owner has five kids—and flashing colored lights. Lucille, the bartender, is wearing a knit cap with reindeer cavorting across it. The Knock-Knock used to be frequented by older people, but now the regulars are edged out, on the weekends, by a younger crowd that's big on neon-colored drinks in mar-tini glasses. Wednesdays are kind of a mix, and not as packed. You can actually hear yourself when you strike up a conversa-tion with somebody.

Around my third Cape Cod a cute boy sits down next to me at the bar, and we end up trying to read each other's palms. I've got my right hand on the bar, and he's tracing it so lightly it tickles, and I keep laughing and snatching it away in between I don't know how many more drinks. We both know where the lifeline is, but neither of us can figure out which of the two horizontal lines is the head, and which is the heart. The one curving around between the thumb and forefinger is a complete mystery. After a while he lets go, and we just sip our drinks while "White Christmas" plays on the jukebox for the millionth time, and he asks if he can walk me home.

The other reason I like the Knock-Knock is that there is a row of bushes en route to my mother's townhouse. That's where this guy and I stop. I shuck my panties and get on my hands and knees, on the strip of grass between the bushes and sidewalk. I pull my long skirt over my head and wait for him to put on the condom. A car goes by and I can feel the headlights spread over me, but my skirt is like a little fort, the kind my good brother and I used to make by hanging blankets over the dining room table, and I don't care if some driver sees a girl's ass, naked, about to be entered by some stranger. The driver could pull over, for all I care, and do what this guy is doing now, grabbing my hips and pushing my face into the smells of earth and grass, doing it fast, either because he's afraid someone will come by or because that's how he likes it. It's over in a couple of minutes.

He stands up. I listen to the sound of his zipper closing, his belt sliding through the buckle.

"You gonna get up?" he says.

"No," I say.

"Okay," he says.

I wait. He stands there a minute more, and then he walks back in the direction of the Knock-Knock. A bug of some kind crawls over the back of my neck, its tiny legs scratching and tickling, and I don't move.

. . .

On the day before Christmas, my mother drives to my bad brother's condo and cleans it because if she didn't, she says, he'd just live in his own mess.

When she gets back to the rink I'm feeling kind of spacey from a codeine my other brother gave me. Even though he's an athlete, he doesn't mind getting high sometimes. He won't give me pills very often because he thinks I might be saving them up. He doesn't know about the Valium. I popped the codeine right in front of him, to reassure him. Now I'm feeling good, and I don't want to be brought down by hearing about my dick of a brother.

"I don't know why you won't try to get along with him," my mother is saying.

I think of the time he took a skate and hit her in the back with it, and she had to get stitches.

"He feels shut out," she says. "He can be such wonderful company, if he's in a good mood."

I busy myself with making fresh coffee, banging the plastic filter on the inside of the trash bin to dump the grounds.

If I want company, I can hang out with my good brother. We go to rock concerts, and out to dinner, or just hang around his apartment watching TV. Sometimes he lets me lean against him and put my head on his shoulder, and he puts his arm across the back of the couch, and I wish someone with magical powers would come along and freeze us in that position so I never had to hear him say, *It's getting late, I've got lessons tomorrow*, and I never had to hear myself say, *Yeah, I guess I'd better go*.

234

"Maybe he could go to college," my mother says. "Lots of adults go to college now. Of course," she says after a minute, "you didn't like it much, did you?"

I didn't apply to any colleges my last year of high school. My father was in the nursing home by then, and my mother was visiting him every day, so she didn't bother me about it. A couple of years later I enrolled at the local junior college. I didn't like the instructors, who lectured on in dry voices, staring at the back wall. The other students were stupid and hadn't read any books. I watched a professor make chalk diagrams on the blackboard, and all I could think about were scratches on ice, and my mother putting out the newsletter, *Let's Skate*, all by herself, and my handsome brother gliding toward some beautiful female student while I was in class. My college career ended after a few weeks, and I had to pay my mother back for the part of the tuition that was nonrefundable.

My good brother comes in with sandwiches from the deli. I open my roast turkey and watch him unwrap the white paper from his ham sandwich and pick up the rye bread and bring it to his mouth. I imagine that the paper is a white dress.

"He needs to snap out of it," my mother says.

• • •

In the afternoon I take off to get us a tree, since it's clear that if I don't we will end up with the decorated fake ficus again. My good brother has lessons, and my mother doesn't want to leave the rink, as usual, so I call my friend Darla, the only friend I still have from high school. Plus her father has a minivan we can borrow. We walk around the lot, and it takes me forever to find the perfect tree. The man at the lot pries it off the wood it's nailed to and helps us get it into the truck. At the town-house we drag it into the living room, but we don't decorate it; I want to save that for tonight.

We're sitting at the kitchen table, drinking egg nog with shots of dark rum, when my bad brother's Camaro squeals into the driveway. He has his own house key. He slams in through the front door and heads downstairs to the rec room, talking to himself a mile a minute. The words are slurred and mumbled, but *whore* is one of them.

Darla looks at me and rolls her eyes.

"The voices," I say, and get up and go to the phone.

"What do they say?" Darla whispers. We can hear him banging things around in the rec room.

"They say, Drop dead. Go kill yourself."

I speed-dial the rink, and my good brother picks up.

"Can you come over?" I ask him. "You-Know-Who is here."

"I can't right now," he says.

"I'm afraid of him." He's dragging something across the room, and I hope he's barricading himself in down there.

"I have to go. Hilda Braun is here." Hilda Braun used to be my mother's student. She was old when she started, and now she's ancient.

"Let Mom take her. Hilda likes taking a lesson with her sometimes."

"I can't," my brother says. "I'll see you later. You'll be okay." He hangs up.

"Promise you'll help me if he tries anything," I say to Darla.

"The voices say, Go drown in the ocean and get eaten by barracudas," she says.

"Go put a gun in your mouth and blow your brains out," I say.

We start laughing, trying to be quiet, but then Darla spits egg nog and we can't stop ourselves.

My brother comes in, barefoot. His feet are filthy. He combs his long-nailed fingers through his hair and stands there staring at us.

"Hey," Darla says nervously.

"Get out," my brother says to me. He starts making little shooing motions with his hands.

"I live here," I say.

"No, you don't," he says. He comes toward me and stands over my chair. "Go away," he says, very softly. Then he puts both hands around my neck, digs his thumbs in, and starts choking me.

I grab his wrists, but I can't break his grip. I kick at his legs and try to step on his bare feet. Darla gets up from her chair and for a second she looks like she's just going to stand there, but then she moves around the table and starts hitting him. When that doesn't do anything she manages to grab him around the waist and pull, and they both stagger backwards.

My brother starts laying into Darla, and soon he's got her down on the kitchen floor. I jump on his back, and he throws me off, and Darla and I end up on the floor while he alternates kicking us in the ribs.

"Out, out, out!" he's screaming, over and over.

"Fuck you," I say, even though I know that will probably make it worse. "I wish you were dead."

He stops then, and looks at me. "I feel dead," he says.

Just when I think he's going to kick me in the head, he runs out of the house.

. . .

"Hey, you," my good brother says, coming into the office with his skates on. The floor is black rubber, made for skate blades; people walk on it all day and never leave a mark. "What did you get Mom for Christmas?"

Our mother is out on the ice. A few easy turns, and then she spins like a ballerina on a jewelry box. The codeine I took after my brother tried to choke me has worn off. I hate the way I feel right now.

"You should have come over," I say. "He attacked me."

"I'm sorry," my brother says. "I can't be there every minute." He comes over and strokes my hair, and I lean my head against his stomach. He smells like cologne and sweat and frozen breath.

"Look, I'm thinking about skipping the Christmas thing tomorrow," he says. "I told Mom I'd cover for her, so she could go home and eat dinner with you guys."

I lean back in the office chair to look in his eyes, but he's gazing out the window, like there's something unusual happening on the ice. But the ice is empty, except for our mother. It's Christmas Eve, and people are home with their families. They're putting tinsel and popcorn balls on their trees. They're spraying their windows with stuff that looks like snow. In the living room there's a piano, and the family gathers around it, singing "Silent Night" and "O Come All Ye Faithful." The father of the family isn't sitting on the couch pissing in an orange juice container, like my father did the Christmas before he died. The oldest son isn't telling the mother that she's a fucking controlling bitch, or screaming at his sister that she's a stupid pig.

"Don't bail on me," I say. "You can't. You have to be there tomorrow. For me. Please."

"Hey, let's skate," he says.

"You know I don't."

"Aw, come on. Maybe it's time you started."

"I can't," I tell him. He's already headed out the door. "Sometimes I want to die," I whisper, but by then he's on the ice.

I watch him circle the rink a couple of times, and then he moves toward my mother in the center, lithe and easy. She extends her hand, and he takes it, and the two of them turn, each on a single skate, each with a leg lifted parallel to the ice.

He left his backpack on the floor by the desk. I go through it and find three Klonopins in an Ibuprofen bottle, and put one in my pocket. I haven't had a Klonopin in years. The last time was at a party we went to together. It was right after high school, after my father died. Sometime during the night I felt my way forward in a dark room and lay down on a bed in a pile of coats and went to sleep. When I woke up my brother was sliding on top of me, and when he touched me between my legs I just opened them. I felt like my true life was beginning, that my brother and I would be together forever, that he was acknowledging the bond between us and would never let me fall. I remember how it felt, sinking deeper into the coats, like sinking down into a river that was gradually freezing over, the music from the party getting fainter and fainter.

I move back to the window to watch the two of them and put my forehead to the glass. It's cold from the chilly air of the rink, like a slab of clear ice lifted up. I make a little skater with my right hand, from my index and middle finger, and she slides around them on the glass. She circles them over and over, hypnotized, until I tell her to quit, until I give her a little push and together we skate away.

ACKNOWLEDGMENTS

Gratitude to the editors of the following publications where these stories first appeared:

"Another Breakup Song"—*Bloom* online

"Beautiful Lady of the Snow"—*Five Points*

"Blown"—*Another Chicago Magazine*

"Breathe"—*New Letters*

"Ever After"—*Fairy Tale Review*

"The Hag's Journey"—*New Ohio Review*

"Ice"—*Mississippi Review*

"In the Time of the Byzantine Empire"—Ducts.org

"Intuition"—*Willow Springs*

"Night Owls"—*Indiana Review*

"Only the Moon"—*Another Chicago Magazine*

ACKNOWLEDGMENTS

"The Other Woman"—*American Short Fiction* online

"The Palace of Illusions"—*Narrative Magazine* online

"Ever After" was featured on NPR's "Selected Shorts" and appears on a CD volume *Selected Shorts: Behaving Badly*. It was also included in the anthology *My Mother She Killed Me, My Father He Ate Me: Forty New Fairy Tales* (Penguin) and in *The Fairy Tale in Popular Culture* (Broadview).

"Ice" received First Prize in the *Mississippi Review* fiction competition.

Grazie: to Jay Schaefer and Darleen Lev, who read endless drafts of stories and taught me how to write them. To Tom Jenks, for generosity and guidance with the title story. To the Civitella Ranieri Foundation, which afforded me the time and inspiration to create new stories after a long hiatus.

ABOUT THE AUTHOR

KIM ADDONIZIO is the author of a previous story collection, *In the Box Called Pleasure*; two novels, *Little Beauties* and *My Dreams Out in the Street*; five poetry collections; and two books on writing poetry. She recently collaborated with woodcut artist Charles D. Jones on *My Black Angel: Blues Poems and Portraits*. She has received numerous honors for her writing, including a Guggenheim Fellowship and two NEA Fellowships, and was a National Book Award Finalist in 2000. She lives in Oakland, CA, and New York City and teaches private writing workshops in person and online. She plays harmonica with the word/music group Nonstop Beautiful Ladies and volunteers for The Hunger Project, a global organization empowering the poorest people in the world to end their own hunger and poverty. Visit her at www.kimaddonizio.com.